Charred Hope

HEART OF FIRE, BOOK THREE

LIZZY FORD

ISBN-13: 978-1-62378-141-5

Dedication

For all the dragon lovers who happily adopted Chase and Skye and made their story so successful!

Chapter One

CHACE COULDN'T SLEEP, even if he wanted to. Every time he tried, his heart thumped so loudly that he wasn't able to fall asleep.

Figures my heart is keeping me awake.

A few weeks before, when he'd had no heartbeat, he'd been thrilled to hear the first thud. Now, it was like a ticking clock, a reminder that time was passing, and he was helplessly watching it run by him. It wasn't just the sound keeping him awake this night, but the pain, too. In the solitude of privacy and beneath the curtain of night, he wasn't able to ignore the ache that pierced him like nothing before ever had. Without his lair, he never really felt safe anymore.

He came here instead to think. Seated on a charred chunk of cement at The Field, he stared into the night sky overhead. It was chilly in the deserts of southern Arizona, but he didn't care. The soft glow of warm light came from the once-magic bar a short distance away, the place they'd hoped to make a stand against the slayers three days before, only discover their issues were much, much worse.

Dragons soared through the night and perched on nearby hills, keeping an eye on the bar and its surroundings, while nocturnal panthers and other great cats loped between the watch points as a secondary layer of defense. Without the magic of the dragon king to protect it, the bar that acted as a refuge for shifters was stranded in the middle of the desert, its location known to all their enemies.

Because I have no power. The thought no longer filled him with anger or sorrow or any other emotion that left him frustrated. He'd spent the past few days getting over his feelings and now focused on how he was going to change things for the better, if it was even possible.

"You keep coming back to this spot," his best friend, Gunner, said, approaching with the silence of the panther shifter he was. He sat down on a piece of the demolished compound nearby.

"I'm missing something," Chace said, gaze dropping from the sky to his surroundings. "It's here. Somewhere." Only dark lumps of melted metal and smashed concrete blocks remained of The Field. They hadn't found as much as a pen that wasn't irreparably damaged, let alone a computer or file cabinet that might offer some clue as to where the slayers' secret location was.

"We've been over the ruins a million times," Gunner said.

"I know." Chace rose and walked a short distance. "There's got to be some clue as to where Mason took her. It's got to be here."

Light from a half moon dusted the dark shapes of saguaro cacti and other bushes around The Field. Nothing stirred, aside from the four-legged sentries circling the small valley.

If you have any sort of mercy, I could use some, he thought at the stars. He missed soaring close to them, peering down at the world.

His eyes closed, and he imagined what it was like to feel the cold air currents ruffle the fur lining his scales and tug at his wings. He yearned to soar in the heavens again, for the sense of freedom he always experienced when he was flying. Fire blazed through his bloodstream when he was in dragon form, and he sought some small trickle of the magic, praying it remained.

It's useless. With a sigh, Chace opened his eyes and focused on the desert. His brow furrowed at what was in front of him. About fifty meters away, a familiar, boxy shape had appeared out of nowhere.

"Cabin?" he asked skeptically. "Is that you?"

One window lit up in response. Chace's heart almost stopped, and he stared, shocked.

"What're you talking about?" Gunner asked, twisting to look in the direction Chace did.

"You don't see it?" Chace asked, doubting his own eyes.

"No. I rarely did, though."

"True." Chace strode forward, his long legs closing the distance to the cabin fast. Taking the steps two at a time, he paused in front of the door, elated to see his long time friend.

His hand shook as it rested on the cold, metal doorknob. He drew a breath to steady his excitement then opened the door.

Abruptly, the cabin disappeared. He fell the few feet to the ground, jarred by the unexpected drop.

Chace caught his balance, puzzled. He'd not only seen the cabin but also touched it. It was real, or had been, for a few seconds at least.

He turned all the way around, spotting the small cabin about a dozen feet away, between him and the hotel.

"Cabin?" he asked again. "What's going on?"

Though it had never spoken to him with words, it always found a way to communicate with him.

This time, the window and the porch light flickered on, as if the cabin was welcoming him.

Chace started forward with more caution. He reached it and climbed one stair, waited, then climbed to the top. After another short pause, he went to the door. The lights stayed on strong, the boards beneath his feet solid. Assured the cabin was real, he opened the door.

And found himself dropping to the ground for a second time.

"What the hell?" Chace grimaced. He spun, eyes falling to the cabin.

All its lights were flashing quickly in a communication he recognized as the lair laughing him.

He ignored Gunner's chuckle.

"You're messing with me, aren't you?" He folded his arms across his chest. "Is that really necessary?"

The lights all flashed brightly then went dark.

"Okay. So ... you're pissed at me." He wiped his mouth. "You gonna tell me why? Or just keep dropping me on my ass?"

The cabin didn't respond.

Damn, moody, passive-aggressive, PMSing cabin. Chace sighed.

"I missed you," he admitted gruffly. "A lot. We've been together for a thousand years. I never knew how ... good that was, until you were gone from my life."

One light came on, as if the magic in the cabin was listening.

"I'm sorry for abandoning you in Oregon. And ... for not thinking of you at all when I traded in my magic. It was a selfish decision, one I've regretted every second of every day since I made it," he continued in a softer tone, troubled. "I really missed you. Not because of everything you've done for me, but because in some really twisted, crazy way, you've been my friend for a thousand years."

The front door creaked open to reveal the familiar, cozy, well-lit interior of his home. Knowing how quickly his cabin changed moods, Chace warily approached and ascended the steps once more. He took a tentative step into the interior.

With relief, he realized the cabin had forgiven him.

Mostly.

All his furniture was rearranged, and it had emptied the contents of all the cupboards and cabinets onto the floor.

He almost ordered it to clean up then realized it wasn't right to take advantage of his friend the way he had his whole life.

"I'll clean up," he said. "Pizza?"

The oven door opened to reveal its glowing interior. The scent of a freshly baked pizza rolled over him. He breathed it in, grinning.

"Thank you," he said. "You're a good friend. A damned moody one, but a good one nonetheless."

The oven snapped shut. Chace ignored the mini hissy fit and went to work cleaning up the mess his cabin left him.

I wish it was this easy to apologize to Skylar.

His gaze lingered on the door, and he wondered again how she was. Where she was. How he was going to find her and help her.

What happened if his magic didn't return, and her luck ran out.

You're a dragon, Chace. Why didn't you help us? Her broken tone and the memory of the hurt in her gaze haunted him every minute of his day. The words played over and over in his mind.

Chace paused in place, kneeling to pick up a roll of trash bags the cabin seemed to be trying to use as a streamer to decorate the place.

"I can see it," Gunner called from the foot of the porch stairs. "I'm afraid it's mad at me, too, or I'd come in."

"Pretty sure it's only mad at me. Come on up," Chace replied.

Gunner did so cautiously and entered. "I'll let you clean up your own mess this time."

Chace shot him a glare.

Gunner grinned and threw himself down in a chair in the living area, content to watch.

The scent of his late night dinner soon filled the air, like it often did. Chace was comforted by the flavorful smell and grateful to set foot again in the cabin that had been his home for so long.

"I told you I needed to be here," Chace said, sorting his belongings into piles.

"Yeah. You were right. Wonder how it found you. You've got no magic, right?"

Chace tested himself. No fire trickled or poured into his blood, and he shook his head. "I don't *feel* it, but I know it's there. I was able to heal myself and Sky. I don't get it."

"Did you ask dragon-daddy at any point?"

Chace didn't answer. Skylar's father, Gavin, had told him what it'd take to regain his magic, and he didn't yet have a clue how to go about winning over the forgiveness of a woman who had too many good reasons to be mad at him.

"Hey, is this yours?"

He looked up at Gunner's curious voice to see his best friend holding up a cell phone. Gunner tapped it, and the screen lit up. A picture of Sky was the wallpaper.

"No." Chace rose, drawn to the image of her smiling. He took the phone and studied it, not recognizing the all-black case or the clothing she wore in the picture. "This picture looks old. I can see The Field in the background."

He unlocked the screen with a swipe of his thumb. Only the basic apps had been installed on the phone, and there was a text message waiting. He tapped the icon.

C- I programed Sky's new number into the phone. I'm not the bad guy here. - Mason

"Mason!" Chace exclaimed, his breath catching. He showed the message to Gunner, who frowned.

"Oy. I do not get a warm fuzzy about that cat," Gunner said. "Why would he do this?"

"If it's real, I don't care." For the second time within ten minutes, Chace's insides trembled with excitement. "First cabin, now Sky."

"Test it first. Make sure it's her that responds."

For a split second, Chace heard the hum of magic in the air around him. He cocked his head to the side, uncertain how to interpret it.

"I think cabin is saying it'll be her," he said. He gazed at the cell phone, not daring to hope he'd soon know how and where Sky was.

"What're you waiting for?" Gunner's amused question pulled him out of his thoughts. "Send her a note."

Chapter Two

SKYLAR SAT UP IN HER NARROW BED, unable to sleep. Starlight slipped through the spaces between the blinds of her small room, and she folded her legs onto the bed. It was warm enough in the hideout located in the mountains of northern Arizona. The setting outside the compound's tall fences was peaceful and quiet, filled with pine trees and a natural lake whose waters were a muddy green during daylight.

Every night since the skirmish between griffins and dragons, nightmares had jarred her out of sleep. She kept witnessing her father fall to his death in an attempt to save her life. Over and over he fell, and over and over she experienced the sense of free falling and despair.

I didn't even really like him. She barely knew him and didn't exactly see eye to eye with him ... but he was the only family she'd ever known. It wasn't easy for her to try to process her emotions. *Chace should've been there for us.*

"That's not true," she whispered into the quiet room. "He lost his magic. He couldn't have helped Gavin, even if he wanted to."

Then what hurt? Her father's death of course. Yet something about Chace hurt, too, and she wasn't able to pinpoint what. She couldn't get Chace's parting words out of her thoughts.

I love you, Sky. Nothing you do or say to me is going to change that, he'd said.

He'd meant it. As flawed as Chace admitted to being, he did love her. Would he be there if she needed him again as promised? Because she sensed the day approaching when she was going to need the backup.

She sighed. Aware she'd get no more sleep this night, she dressed quickly and left her room, exiting into a long hallway lit by fluorescent lighting.

There were many mysteries about the compound she hadn't been able to figure out. The most important one: why they let her roam around without restriction. Mason, her slayer-turned-shifter quasi-friend, said he trusted her to remain with them until she'd learned what he needed her to.

She did stay, and a part of her thought it was as much because she needed to uncover what was going on as it was because she had nowhere else to go.

Leaving the barracks, she tugged on a jacket and walked out into the quiet night. Within the compound was a small picnic area where she'd found the perfect table to sit on to look out over the lake. The air smelled of pine trees and muddy water, and a cool breeze tickled the back of her neck.

A tingle went through her, an indication that a shifter was close. She'd been growing more aware of them as the days passed, able to pick up the individual signatures of shifter magic as the creatures moved around the compound.

"I keep forgetting cats are nocturnal," she murmured.

"Your ability to sense us is getting stronger." Mason's dark purr came from nearby.

You have no idea. In the three days she had spent at Mason's compound, she'd been surrounded by shifters all day, every day. She could not only sense them around her, but she'd begun to identify which shifter it was. It was instinctive, like a tiny whisper that came from the depths of her soul. Not only did she know their names before she saw or spoke to them; she also knew what kind of animal or creature they shifted into. It was a gift stemming from her role as the Protector of shifters.

For someone who spent most of her adult life capturing and caging shifters, she wasn't certain how to view her awakening gift or the responsibility that came with it, especially when she had no shifter magic of her own. In the past, every Protector had a champion – a dragon of immense power, capable of enforcing order among the shifters.

Her champion had no power. She had no influence or knowledge about how to use her emerging skills.

The world she was supposed to protect was about to plunge into civil war, one that would threaten the human population as well as potentially wipe out the shifters.

And I'm supposed to fix this? Not for the first time, she grew angry with her deceased father for taking his secrets to the grave.

"You haven't answered my question, Sky," Mason said, drawing her attention from her thoughts.

She twisted to see him. His skin was as dark as night, the same color of his fur, when he shifted into his black lion form. She wanted to trust him. Wanted to trust *someone* after her world was turned on its head.

But Mason?

"It's none of your business, Mason," she replied.

"We've been friends for a few years, and it's none of my business if you're okay?" There was familiar frustration in his voice.

"Friends don't betray friends."

"I did my best to protect you along the way."

"I know. I can see that in my dreams," she said, meeting his dark gaze. "I don't know what to think about that either. You knew I was brainwashed, went along with it for six years. I don't really feel like thanking you right now."

"I get it." Mason took a deep breath. "I don't blame you. This didn't end up how it was supposed to, though." He moved silently to the picnic table and sat beside her.

"You killed Dillon's dad. What did you expect would happen?" she asked. "He's always been on the edge of snapping."

"I know." Mason appeared troubled. "You haven't said anything about ... you know. My shifter ability."

"I thanked you for helping defend us," she said. "I don't know what to think about everything yet, Mason, including what you want me to do. If what you say is correct, and this war between griffins and dragons has returned, I don't think it's possible for you and the other slayers to play nicely with the shifters. You've done too much damage caging them over the years, especially with the dragons."

"I can hope."

She studied him, saddened that her friend had kept so much from her. Mason had taken care of her in more ways than she knew over the years, but she wasn't able to overlook the pain of his betrayal and all he'd hidden from her.

"Maybe not hope," he added. "Maybe ... make amends is a better phrase."

"You can start by answering *my* questions!"

"Too dangerous."

She rolled her eyes. "Then why do you think I'd ever trust you again?"

"We have a common purpose."

"Getting rid of Dillon."

"I was thinking more along the lines of protecting you from him. He knows your value."

"I have *no* value!" she snapped and rose, pacing. "What would he do with me, aside from snap me in two? He can't use me to exert control over the shifter community, because I have no idea how to do anything!"

"That's always been the plan, though," Mason said quietly.

Skylar faced him, hands on her hips. She eyed him.

"Well ... you wanted the truth, didn't you?" Mason chuckled. "My boss hasn't changed her mind. I doubt Dillon will either. The first attempt to control the shifters through selectively capturing those deemed strong enough to resist and controlling you failed miserably. You freed those we spent years collecting. We wiped your mind, and yet you still remember."

"Lucky me," she said. "It's all about power and control."

"Isn't everything?"

"See, that's where you're so far off, Mason. What about friendship or love or simply living in peace with one another?" she insisted.

He shrugged. "Maybe. But I'd still rather be on the winning side in the end. I think it can be done differently."

"No matter who gets hurt in the process."

"I'm not like Dillon. I'd never hurt you."

"You *did* hurt me." She pointed out. "But whatever. I'm a mythical Protector, which somehow makes me worth killing for. I'm assuming your boss won't let me leave here, either, will she?"

Mason smiled but didn't answer.

"And who is this mysterious boss of yours?"

Another amused silence.

"Right. Then why am I here?"

"Your kind comes along once every few thousand years. Gavin waited five thousand years for your mother. The fact there were two born within decades of one another is incredible. Your kind only appear when they're needed most," Mason explained. "It doesn't bode well for the shifters. It means you're meant to complete the mission your mother wasn't able to."

"So she is dead." Skylar's hopes of discovering more about her mother tumbled.

"I don't think you'd be coming into your power if not."

"You know more, don't you?"

"Not my place to say."

Skylar rubbed her face, gaze drifting again to the lake beyond the chain-link fence of the compound

"What next, Mason?" she asked. "We've been here three days! What are you waiting for?"

11

He held out his hand.

She eyed it. "New method of brainwashing people?"

"No, Sky," he said with a sigh. "We're waiting for your magic to emerge. We can't track Dillon, but you can."

"I can?"

He waved his hand.

She stepped forward and took it.

"Think of Dillon. You don't understand your senses yet but I might be able to using my magic. As our Protector, you can locate any shifter anywhere. It's one of the reasons why everyone is afraid of you."

Skylar closed her eyes, anger fluttering through her as she thought of Dillon. Whereas Chace's magic was like a bonfire roaring through her body, Mason's was faint, a cool stream.

"Okay, good. You're definitely stronger than you were three days ago," Mason said. "Concentrate."

She did, her anger solidifying at the image of Dillon in her mind. She didn't understand what it was Mason was doing, and she didn't hear the quiet whisper that might tell her where Dillon was.

"Almost." Mason released her hand. His magic faded. "I think maybe …" He rose and gazed at the lake. "Well, I'm wondering if your kind –"

"*Stop* calling me that!" she said through clenched teeth. "You have any idea how rude that is?"

He considered her for a moment. "Sorry. Okay, I'm wondering if the Protectors chose dragons for a secondary reason, not just because they're typically the strongest shifters. Dragons love mountains, and the old legends about your … um, women with your gifts say you lived in mountains, too."

"You think I can mentally *see* or whatever better from a mountain top?" she asked curiously. "I have no real affinity for mountains. Should I?"

"Beats me." He leapt off the table. "But we can try it. There is a danger though. All shifters can sense their Protector and her guardian. So if you can find Dillon, he might be able to find you, too."

"Good. I'd like to tell him to go to hell in person then lasso his ass." She'd kept one lasso with her, just in case she needed to use it on someone like Mason.

Skylar looked around the compound. They were nestled in a valley, overlooking the lake, tucked beneath the main peaks of the mountains. No part of her wanted to climb a damn mountain to find someone like Dillon.

What if I can find Chace, too? Was it possible to locate any shifter anywhere?

Did she want to, after walking away from him?

She grappled with the answer for a moment before deciding that yes, she did. Even if she hadn't yet fully forgiven him, she needed to know he was safe. After all, in human form, he was as vulnerable to someone like Dillon as she was.

"With all these shifters around, I'm tempted to say I don't want to climb," she said, unimpressed with the distance. "I'm guessing it's a two day walk."

"We've got a couple Pegasus' and a Sphinx shifter here. Let me see who's available. Cats hate flying." His last statement was disgruntled. He started away then stopped, facing her again. "Call this an act of good faith."

He tossed her a cell phone. She gazed down at it, puzzled.

This is so not normal. When he disappeared into the building, she unlocked the screen.

She had a message. Was it for her? What did he mean about act of good faith?

The contact's name was listed as *Chace.*

Skylar's heart flipped over in her chest and she sucked in a breath, holding it. Anticipation raced through her, and she hesitated, afraid of being devastated, if it wasn't from him. With eagerness she didn't want to feel, she opened the message, giddiness filling her when she realized it really was Chace.

Are you okay? The text read. Deceptively simple, measured, guarded. "Definitely Chace," she murmured. She debated how to answer.

Yeah. You? She typed. She hit the send button, dissatisfied with the message when there was so much more to say.

His response was quick. *Yeah. Cabin says hi.*

She smiled, unexpected warmth and emotion blooming within her. She'd always liked Chace's cabin, and she suspected the cabin liked her, too. It was nice to know Chace wasn't alone now. He had his old friend back at least.

"What about your magic?" she asked the phone. The question seemed too personal for their tenuous exchange. She typed a different text instead.

Hello to cabin. Hope she's setting you straight.

After an internal debate, she tucked the phone away in her pocket again.

"Got us a ride!" Mason called, striding out of the barracks.

A man dressed in pajama bottoms with mussed hair trailed him, blinking rapidly, as if Mason just shook him awake.

"I guess we'll give it a try," she said, still uncertain what to think of Mason and what he admitted to wanting.

What happened if she succeeded in being able to locate shifters? Was Mason setting her up once more with the intention of using her? Was it better not to admit she had the gift, even if it worked, if it meant protecting the others?

Her gaze lingered on the dark forms of the peaks above. *I need to learn how to protect those that need it.* Even if it meant playing Mason's game. For now.

Chapter Three

AN HOUR LATER, SHE RELEASED Mason and slid off the back of the largest horse she'd ever seen. The Pegasus was black from head to wings to tail, and the flight was far smoother than she expected.

The winged horse folded its wings and walked to the edge of the plateau where he'd dropped them off, the highest point they were able to reach that had a ledge large enough to hold them and any potential winged visitors, like nocturnal dragons, who found them.

Skylar pulled her knit cap over her ears. The air of the peaks was cold, and she pushed her hands into her pockets.

Mason went to the edge of the plateau and gazed out over the peaks, saddles and valleys below them. He was quiet. She joined him.

"Cats hate flying," he sat at last, a grimace on his face.

She smiled, somewhat satisfied to know he was as much outside his comfort zone as she was.

"Can you sense anything?" he asked.

"I don't even know how," she admitted.

"You can feel when one of us is near you and know our names, right?"

She eyed him.

"I felt it when my magic was in you," he said with a smile. "Can you feel anything else right now?"

"I don't think so." She turned her focus internal and listened for the instinct that was humming with the nearness of Mason and the Pegasus. "What should I be doing to sense them?"

He shrugged. "You're the Protector."

Gee, thanks. She blew out a frustrated breath.

"Maybe it takes a little while?" he asked, inquisitive gaze on her.

"How would I know?" she shot back.

"Fair enough. Want me to call the boss up to see if she'll meet with us while we're waiting?"

"Absolutely," Skylar said, surprised he was offering after avoiding the topic for days. "I get to meet the mysterious figure behind this mess at last!"

"She's a dragon, so ..." He cleared his throat. "I think you know what that means in terms of moodiness."

"Bring it. You all need me for some reason, so I've got nothing to fear."

"Always so optimistic." Mason pulled out his phone and texted someone quickly.

Skylar found herself reaching for the cell he gave her to see if Chace responded. She was pleased to see he had.

Cabin always liked you more than me anyway.

She smiled. "Mason, why did you do this?" She held up the phone.

"I told you," he said, glancing up from his text. "I'm not your enemy, Sky."

"You're a funny kind of ally, though," she said. "You want to use me to control the shifters. My whole life was wiped out for this purpose."

"Second chances," he whispered. "This is mine."

"To do what? You seem to be after the same thing you were before!"

"I don't want you hurt. Or miserable. Or brainwashed. I want you to be who you need to be," he said in clear aggravation. "Whatever form that takes. Even if you and my boss disagree."

"So ... what? You're sticking around to protect me?"

"Until Chace can, yes."

"Interesting." She gazed up at him, sensing truth in his words but not wanting to admit it after all he'd done to help destroy her world.

"Winning team." He rolled his eyes. "She'll be here soon."

Damn dragons. Always interfering with my life. She'd thought Chace was the first to mess with her, only to uncover the interference of Gavin and now the mysterious boss of Mason and Dillon.

"You seem nervous about this, Mason," she observed, watching him pace.

"Dragons aren't my favorite shifters. Too prone to emotional reactions. Not always easy to reason with."

"Tell me about it."

"I have a feeling she's not happy about Dillon going off the reservation. There was a time when she only spoke to him. She's had to work with me the past week or so instead."

"Oh, she might be pissed at the fact I'm not as brainwashed as you wanted," Skylar added sarcastically.

He gave her a long look but didn't respond.

She felt the tingle of fire in her blood before she saw the dragon. Skylar's attention went to the night sky, where she waited to see some movement above them. At last, she saw it, a massive silver-white dragon circling the plateau.

Freyja. The name came to her before the dragon was halfway to the peak.

"Seriously. This chic is emo," Mason warned. "Just play ... nice."

"I know how moody dragons are," she responded. "You all want me alive, so I really am not feeling like playing at all."

The dragon grew nearer, its size seeming to increase as it did. Several minutes later, it alighted on the other end of the plateau.

Skylar gazed at it in fascination, entranced by the shimmer of her silvery wings. The dragon changed shapes, morphing quickly into a naked human form, that of a tall, willowy woman with blonde hair and light eyes.

Mason trotted to her and tossed her a small pack, turning away to give her some privacy to change.

Skylar didn't bother, unconcerned with showing any kind of respect to the mastermind behind the slayers. The reality of what she was doing – who she was meeting – made her heart feel heavy. If not for this dragon, she would've had a normal childhood.

My mother and father would still be alive.

For the first time in three days, she realized she didn't have the lasso with her. She'd been too distracted by texting Chace to run inside and get it before Mason brought out the Pegasus shifter. This was one bitch she hoped to lock up forever, after she learned what she needed to know.

The graceful dragon shifter was sharp of eye, and she seemed to float in the simple jeans and jacket rather than walk. Mason trailed his mistress, appearing tense.

Skylar waited for the woman to approach. She clasped her hands behind her back to keep from throwing something at the dragon shifter.

The beautiful woman stopped a short distance from her, taking her in critically.

"You look more like your mother than your father," she observed.

"Seeing as how I'm not a fan of dragons, I'll take that as a compliment," Skylar replied with more calm than she felt. "I understand you're the person behind the slayers."

The dragon shifter didn't appear pleased. "Means to an end. We didn't hurt any of the shifters, until Dillon and Caleb went off the deep end," the woman said. "What is your name?"

"Skylar."

"I'm Freyja."

"I know."

"You're getting stronger. Good." By Freyja's tone, she really didn't find her observation pleasing.

Skylar wanted to say so many things to the woman who erased

her life, but at the moment, she had the urge to test her ability to draw on shifter magic instead. To see if she could control the dragon before her, the way Mason said she could.

She concentrated hard on pulling the warmth of dragon fire into her body, to soak up what she was able to and see what it let her do.

"Your kind always did push the limits," Freyja said, gaze narrowing. "Maybe it's a good thing you're weak, even if you can't help us find Dillon."

"I really wish I had a lasso right now," Skylar replied. "I'm curious. What was your plan for me, assuming your brainwashing worked?"

Freyja glanced at Mason.

"It didn't, so it no longer matters," the dragon shifter replied with some indignation.

"What did you do to my mother?"

"I see Mason has been talking more than I'd prefer."

"Maybe he thinks I have a right to know what happened to me and my family, why we were sacrificed for some plan to takeover the shifter community."

"To keep it *safe*!" Freyja hissed.

"To start a second war!"

Freyja's face flushed, and the fire in her pupils made her eyes glow. With strength that caught Skylar off guard, the enraged dragon shifter snatched her by the throat and hauled her to the edge of the ledge, dangling her over the nothingness below.

Skylar managed a strangled laugh. "I've been … held over a cliff by a better dragon than … you!"

"Shut up, Sky," Mason said, taking Freyja's arm. "Let's remember that we need the Protector alive."

"Drop … me," Sky insisted. She struggled to breathe but wasn't about to back down.

Freyja's eyes sparked brighter.

"*Alive*," Mason countered.

Freyja growled deep in her chest and retreated from the edge, throwing Skylar down.

She laughed loudly. "You dragons are all the same! All fire, no bite."

Freyja started to shift involuntarily, too irritated to control it.

"Would you stop, Sky?" Mason said in frustration. "You got to meet the boss. Yes, Freyja, she's getting stronger, but she can't find Dillon yet. I think she might need to be up here in the mountains for her gift to awaken fully, since she is the daughter of a dragon."

Freyja shook out her arms, turning away from Skylar.

Skylar climbed to her feet. Mason was tense, Freyja angry. Seeing the dragon that ruined her life upset didn't give Skylar any of the satisfaction she'd hoped for. If anything, she felt worse, knowing her family had been sacrificed to start a war by someone who didn't seem remotely remorseful.

"She does not leave this peak until she can find Dillon," Freyja snarled at Mason. She stalked away, the clothing on her body shredding as she morphed into her dragon form. Without so much as a look back, she took off into the sky.

Skylar watched, amazed by the dragon's effortless climb into the heavens.

"Nice, Sky. You just screwed up any chance you had of getting real answers," Mason snapped.

"She's afraid of me," Skylar replied. "Everything else will fall into place." Despite the words, she wasn't confident after her exchange with Freyja. She hadn't learned anything else about the parts of her life that were erased.

But what exactly do I want to learn that I don't already know? Was it knowledge or her memories returned that she really wanted? *What happened to my mother? That's the only thing I need to know.*

"Now you sound like Gavin," Mason said.

"I'm beginning to think he knew a thing or two about dealing with dragons. I don't think they know the difference between fear and respect."

"And there goes our ride."

She looked towards the Pegasus, who was taking flight as well.

"So you got no answers about your past and no ride back to the base," Mason said. "Did this go the way you wanted?"

"Not really," Skylar admitted. "I don't think you guys can give me back my memories, can you?"

He shook his head.

"And you either don't know or won't say what happened to my mother."

"Caleb and Dillon handled your mother. I've got to assume that she didn't survive," was the quiet response.

"And I dated Dillon for a few months." Skylar shivered. She rubbed her arms, feeling ill at the idea that her former lover had a hand in killing her mother. "I need to find him."

"Settle in then. I have a feeling it's not as easy as flipping a switch." Mason retreated from the edge of the plateau to settle between a couple of boulders against a wall. It was as close to shelter as they'd get on the mountain.

Skylar stayed in place, pensive. "Maybe she's right. Maybe I need to stay here until my gift awakens. The idea that I become the Protector I should be is what scares her, isn't it?"

"Possibly. No one living has ever seen a Protector. Gavin was the oldest shifter, the only who might've been old enough to know what a Protector is capable of. What we know is mainly myth and legend," Mason replied. "No one knows what your mother's gift was. It seems like every Protector in the stories has a different type of talent."

She drew nearer as he spoke.

"I don't know for sure, but I don't think your mother would've been susceptible to being kidnapped by shifters, if she'd had time for her gift to awaken."

"She was with my father for almost fifteen years," Skylar said with a frown. "Are you saying we're stuck on this mountain top for fifteen years?"

"God, I hope not. Maybe she was not strong enough to be what you could be," he said. "Or ... maybe she didn't have the need or motivation to find her inner gift."

"Or maybe my father really didn't know what a Protector was capable of either. I can't imagine he'd leave her defenseless, if she was able to control shifter magic, like he said she should've been," she voiced.

"He didn't know those after her were shifters."

"True," she said with a frown. ""How many of the slayers are actually shifters? And how many are the children of shifters?"

"Most are griffin shifters like Dillon, with a few random shifters like me who were drawn into the idea of creating a more evolved order for the community. There was no Protector for five thousand years, long enough for the shifters to become restless and doubtful such a person even existed. They began to doubt Gavin, too, who was more content to stay in his lair. He really wasn't interested in leading the community."

"I can see that," she murmured, dwelling on what she knew of the reclusive, anti-social blue dragon.

"A few slayers have been the children of shifters, like you, who showed some kind of skill at tracking shifters. They were taken and brainwashed," he said. "Unlike you, the others will never know who they're supposed to be."

"Because you interfered with what they were trying to do to me before my mind was able to be permanently wiped."

"Yep."

She shivered, aware of how close she'd been to having no mind or memories of her own. The cold air of the mountains sank into her clothing, and she squeezed beside him between the boulders.

"You are serious about caring for me, even if you've screwed up my life," she observed. "I'm finding that to be a common trend among the men I trust."

Mason chuckled.

Skylar pulled her knees to her chest and wrapped her arms around them. *I can't wait fifteen years for my gift to emerge.*

"Protectors can use the magic of the nearest shifter," she said, repeating what she'd learned from her father before his death. "What do you think that means? I can make you shift involuntarily?"

"You do that already with dragons."

"Seriously, Mason."

"Skylar, I don't know."

"You're a *shifter!* I'm looking for feedback from someone in the community. What can you do with your magic that I might be able to siphon off you?"

He was quiet for a moment. "Well … in human form, we retain many of the senses of the animal or creature we turn into. I can smell food twenty miles away and see almost a mile out."

"Okay. I don't think sniffing out a pizza will do anything for me. What else can you do?"

"In lion form, I'm a fucking stud. Strongest of the cat shifters. I can jump fifteen feet straight up and survive a thirty-foot fall. Fearless in battle, natural leader, capable of overpowering just about anything, including small dragons."

"Hmmm. So how would I use that?"

Another silence, then, "Sky, what if he means that you can shift into anything that you're near? You can take my magic, shift into a cat bigger and badder than me, and then use that inherent knowledge and power to kick my ass?"

"I don't want to be a shifter," she muttered. "You guys are just walking train wrecks."

"But think about it. What else would Freyja be afraid of?" he insisted.

"Maybe I can just take her magic away."

"The lasso can do that."

"Gavin said that was the role of the Protector's mate, the dragon king. He enforced the laws internally while the Protector defended them."

"How else would you defend the community? Think about it. If you were the scariest mother fucker out there, who would mess with the community?"

"You think I can shift?" she asked skeptically. "Wouldn't Gavin have said, *hey, Sky, you can shift into anything you want?*"

"He said you could use the magic of any shifter against them."

"Maybe I can just make them shift into a human form."

"Before they eat you?"

She rolled her eyes, not wanting to think she was one of *them*. It was more than her brainwashed history of believing herself to be in charge of capturing them. It was her natural aversion to a race of creatures that seemed to be only interested in themselves.

"Think about it. Freyja is *afraid* of you, or maybe what you're becoming. What if it's because she knows you can kick her ass, if she can't control you?"

"Mason, I'm listening. But doesn't it seem far fetched? Doesn't it seem like my mother – the last Protector – would've had the ability to protect me and herself by shifting?" she objected in frustration.

"Maybe there isn't one answer to all that's happened. I don't know. I don't think you should rule this out, though."

"What the hell do I do with that knowledge?"

"Test it. Try to shift."

"That's ridiculous."

He pushed her. "Try it."

"Like I have any idea how to do that!" *And it looks so damn painful ...*

"Give me your hand." He pulled her arm free from her grip around her knees to grab her hand. "I know you can feel my magic. What if you just let it ... I don't know. Maybe you can suck it up like you're a vacuum and then tell yourself to shift."

She almost laughed.

"Look, not to worry you, but I don't want to be on the top of this mountain if your locator gift kicks in and Dillon can find you. We've got about an hour until sunrise. Freyja will go into hibernation for the day, and we'll be exposed until nightfall."

Good point. "Seeing as how I can't use my magic GPS locator right now anyway ..." She sighed. "Your Pegasus won't come back for us?"

"Dragons are moody and Pegasus' are free spirits who like to sleep in," he grumbled. "Who knows? Besides, maybe what you need is like a supercharge of shifter magic to wake up yours. Protectors are coupled with the strongest shifters for a reason. What if Chace's magic being asleep has made yours dormant, too?"

Skylar was quiet. *What if mine waking up helps him, too?* Did she want that? There was a part of her that didn't feel ready to forgive him for all he'd done to mess up her life. Another tiny voice in her mind wanted to help him become the man she knew he could be.

"All right. I'll try it," she said reluctantly. "What do I do?"

"Let's move away from these rocks." He got to his feet and walked towards the edge again. Mason sat down.

Skylar trailed, her stomach turning over. Was she ready for this? To *shift* of all things?

She knelt in front of him.

"Not to sound fresh, but I'm thinking we need to take off our clothes. In case it works," he said.

She rolled her eyes. "You've been after me since I dated Dillon."

Mason gave a sigh. "Yeah, well … we see what happened there." He peeled off his shirt and jeans, folding them to place in a pile nearby, but left on his boxers.

Skylar hesitated then followed his lead, skeptical that she was able to shift and more concerned about freezing to death in the time it took for them to test his theory. She stripped out of her warm clothing down to her bra and underwear then returned to her spot, kneeling in front of him.

"We better hurry." Already, her teeth were chattering, her body starting to shake from cold.

Mason took her hands. "Okay. Close your eyes and focus. You recall what I looked like?"

"Yeah, sure."

"Maybe focus on that image or something. Oh, and pulling in all my magic."

"Alrighty." Unconvinced, she nonetheless closed her eyes and envisioned the massive lion she'd seen last near The Field, when Mason had shifted and was shredding any griffin that got too close to the ground. Powerful and huge, he'd been larger than a horse and far more deadly than a normal giant cat.

Like before, his magic trickled into her body. It was light and cool, making her even colder. She willed more of it into her body without understanding what to do with it. When she siphoned energy out of Chace, it seemed to calm him, to prevent him from changing into a dragon when his emotions got the best of him. There was a purpose to it.

With Mason ... the unfamiliar magic just seemed to float around aimlessly inside her. She kept pulling, the whisper of her instincts growing more vocal with the more she pulled into her.

His name, his shifter family, his age ... it was telling her everything about him, to include the fact that he really had lost a sister when he was young to where he was born – deep in Africa to a poor villager who sold him to another tribe as a laborer when he was old enough. She watched the whole of his history unfold, stunned to learn so much about him in such a short period of time. Just as quickly, the memories faded and disappeared.

The trickle of magic turned to a stream then to a flood. Suddenly, it felt like there was no division between them at all. She was smelling the mix of pine and freedom he did, mixed with a very distant scent of raw meat, birds, and other small animals he was able to prey on.

He's hungry, she realized with a smile.

He was mentally tracking a kill, aware of every small sensation in the world around him. The brush of pine trees against his fur, the scent of fur and earth and forest, and the flick of his ears in any direction where he heard a sound.

Distant pain pierced her quickly enough for her to gasp. It was unlike anything she'd ever felt before: sharp, hot and lingering. It started in her feet and hands, and she opened her mouth in a scream that didn't come out.

Was it her pain or his? Within seconds, it had become fiery agony that swept through her, too deep and fast for her to move. Her insides were twisting, her skin snapping under the duress of muscles that were warping ...

Before she fell unconscious, she began to think this was what it felt like when one of them shifted.

Chapter Four

SKYLAR AWOKE WARM AND COZY. Her nostrils were filled with the scent of fur, earth and early morning.

I didn't know morning had a smell. She wriggled her nose.

It took more effort than usual to pry one eye open then the other, and she found herself squinting at the sky. The peak where she'd spent the night faced west, for which she was grateful. It seemed too bright for her to be up otherwise.

At least I'm warm. Skylar lifted her head to look around.

"Good morning, sunshine." Mason squatted in front of her. He was grinning widely.

Skylar eyed him, not feeling anywhere near as cheerful to be awake so early. Mason's scent was thick in her nostrils, and she resisted the urge to sneeze, not wanting to be rude. She didn't recall him smelling so strong either. It wasn't a bad scent, just the smell of a man.

"You're going to freak a little, so listen close," he started. "Whatever happened last night, it worked. But, I want you to focus on staying calm."

She opened her mouth to ask what the hell he was talking about. The sound of a deep growl emerged.

Startled, she looked around, past the body of a massive lioness she didn't recall being on the ledge with them to the rocky wall of the peak. She opened her mouth to ask Mason what was going on.

Again, the growl emerged.

Oh, shit. Skylar looked down at herself. She took in the massive paws and their claws, the long, sinewy legs and thick, black fur covering her body.

Mason rubbed her on the head, tweaking one of her ears. She swiped at him with a huge paw, but he danced away deftly.

Climbing to her feet, she tested her new body by pacing a short distance away and was amazed at how effortlessly she moved. She felt as strong as Mason appeared in his lion form.

Do I have a tail? She turned, catching a glimpse of it, then began circling, trying to catch it.

"Omigod, Sky, stop!" Mason was laughing so hard, he'd doubled over.

She stopped chasing her tail and gave a long yowl of complaint, unable to figure out how she'd been turned into a giant cat or what to do now that she had.

He dropped to his knees, unable to stop laughing. She nudged him with her massive head, bowling him over. Mason held up his hands as she pawed at him.

"Okay, okay!" he said, reining in his amusement. He shoved her back.

Skylar sat on her haunches, trying hard not to panic.

"Where to start ..." Mason stood once more. "You shifted last night. Had I known it would work, I would've warned you. It's *painful.* You get used to it after enough times but when you're new at shifting, it feels like you're being shredded from the inside out."

She bared her teeth at him.

"So you passed out and finished shifting then just ... slept," he finished. "I think it's a good thing. It got down close to freezing last night. I shifted just to keep warm."

She had the urge to pace or run or hunt or something. The animal instincts weren't hers, and neither was she able to fully figure out

29

what they were. She recognized Mason as being a fellow lion, but the idea of a griffin passing low enough for her to slash its wings with her paw and drag it down for a messy, bloody kill …

She yowled again.

Mason smiled. "If you shifted into a lion, you can shift back," he reasoned. "Do you feel the magic still?"

Skylar rose and walked the length of the ledge, striding back and forth, wishing she had the space to run somewhere and that she wasn't stuck on a mountain.

"Focus, Skylar," Mason called. "Do you feel the magic?"

Even if she did, did she really want to feel that pain again? The creatures made it look so simple to change forms, when she'd just experienced how awful it really was.

"Sky! Focus."

She turned to face Mason again. He was having trouble hiding his amusement.

"Find the magic. Tell it to turn you back."

She continued to pace but sought out the cool thrum of magic in her blood.

Turn me back! She screamed internally.

Pain shot through her.

She froze. Her tail twitched, and she twisted to face it again, fascinated by the appendage that almost seemed independent.

"Concentrate," Mason urged her.

She turned away from her entrancing tail and focused on the magic in her blood. The more she did, the greater the pain became. She sat on her haunches then lowered herself to her belly, leery of the edge of the peak a few feet away. The harder she thought about shifting, the hotter the pain got.

"Shift fast. The faster, the less painful," Mason advised, squatting a short distance from her. "Come on, Sky. You can do it."

She growled at him.

The fire grew and with it the agony. Skylar grated her teeth and closed her eyes, willing the pain to be over quickly. Her skin began to ripple as the bones and muscle beneath took on a different shape, while she felt the fur retract into her body.

Her senses grew duller, until she was no longer able to smell the world around her, aside from pine trees, and the cold wind brushed her skin. There was a snap of pure anguish and then it was gone.

Skylar sagged against the ground, gasping and shaking. She lifted her head from the cold stone beneath her. Her dark hair fell in ringlets to her human arms.

"Oh, thank god!" she breathed.

"Welcome back," Mason said with another laugh.

"You are a dick, Mason."

He said nothing.

Shivering, she accepted her clothing from him with a glare, vowing to whack him with a huge paw when she had the chance. Skylar pulled on her clothes but still couldn't get warm. Her fur had trapped her body heat and kept her comfortable. A coat seemed … flimsy in comparison.

She sat and hugged her knees to her chest.

"So now for the real test," Mason said. "Did that do anything to help you sense others?"

"That was insane," she whispered. "Was I really a lion?"

"Yeah. A huge one."

"Bigger than you?"

"Almost. If you knew what you were doing, you'd do some serious damage," he responded. "I think it's safe to say we cracked the code."

"Oh, god," she said, ducking her face to hide it from the chilly wind. "That was awful."

"It's not *awful*. Your gift is amazing," he corrected. "C'mon. Give me a few more minutes before you give up on being a shifting queen."

She didn't answer but concentrated once more on her ability to locate others. They Protector senses were stronger. She was able to identify Mason faster and …

There were others, like blips on a radar screen. They were everywhere.

"Yeah," she said. "I can sense them. Well, some of them. Maybe close ones?"

"Awesome. Who you got?"

"I'm really hungry, Mason."

"Shifting does that. It's really taxing on the body. You get used to the hunger, too."

She rolled her eyes, beginning to understand why Chace was always in a foul mood if he was always hungry. She sighed and tried to identify whose signatures she was picking up.

"I think the people at your compound," she said. "There are like twelve of them. I can't tell who they are yet. There are another six east of here."

"Where?"

She pointed vaguely over her head. "East. As far as your people are, I think."

"What else?"

"There are more …" She puzzled over the sensations, like small bursts of warm and cool in her thoughts. "I don't know. But there are more. In the mountains."

"Two kinds of creatures like mountains: dragons and griffins." The concern in Mason's voice made her look up.

"I can't tell what they are," she admitted.

"Can you tell *where* they are?"

"Not far." She shrugged.

"Hmmm." He was pensive for a moment. "There's a chance that everyone you can locate, can also sense you."

"Oh, god, I'm so tired!" she said and drew a deep breath. "Are we stuck here until night fall?"

"Or later. When you piss off a woman like Freyja, there's no telling when she intends to come back."

"What's her deal anyway?"

"I imagine there's some jealousy involved. She dated Chace for a while."

"For reals?"

"Yeah."

"So I stole her man *and* I can shift into a dragon bigger than her?" Skylar started to smile despite her exhaustion. "That makes me happy. The minute I'm close enough to steal her magic, I'm so kicking her ass."

"Nice. You don't want to find Dillon or defend the shifters. You want to put the smack down on Chace's ex." Mason shook his head.

"The dragon that took away my family? You can deal with Dillon. You made that mess," she snapped.

"The shifters need a Protector, someone who can keep people like Dillon and Freyja from hurting the community."

She ignored him. Even if he was right, she couldn't help thinking she'd love taking care of Freyja a little too much.

"My only question is this: do I need to be touching a shifter to steal its magic?" she mused aloud.

"Why don't we try it a few times?" he suggested.

She flinched, recalling the pain.

"You've always been the bravest person I've known, Skylar. Don't chicken out now. It's exhausting and painful, but if you can get it down where you can shift out of instinct, you will be so far ahead of everyone you run across," Mason said.

She nodded. Her thoughts went to her mother, and she wondered again why Ginger had never learned to shift. Did Gavin keep it from her, or did he not know? She felt guilty thinking badly of him, if he didn't know, and even worse knowing her mother could've survived, if she had learned to shift in time.

Maybe she was too busy with me to try.

Guilt raced through her at the idea she'd somehow prevented her mother from escaping or hiding. The more she learned about who she was, the murkier the circumstances around her mother's disappearance became. Did any one person know what actually happened that day six years ago, when Caleb came to get her?

Chapter Five

"**Y**OU'RE SURE ABOUT THIS?" Chace paused to steady his breathing. Leaning back in his harness, he eyeballed Gunner, who was a much slower climber than he was. Shortly after midnight, Gunner had sprung out of his seat with the wild claim that he knew where Skylar was.

"I can't explain it," Gunner said with a grunt. "Just bam! I could pick her up. And you."

If Cabin hadn't acted on his friend's words, Chace might've doubted it was possible. "Dragon daddy said the shifters could sense the Protector and her dragon. It just seems odd that it kicked I like that."

"Yeah, well, it works."

"Why now?"

"Like I have any idea."

Chace smiled. He tried to imagine Gunner working as a doctor in a hospital with his abrupt, surly bedside manner. After being a patient to the panther shifter that had no mercy on someone in pain, he didn't think Gunner had lasted long in that line of work.

Or maybe it was just me he treats like that. Like cabin throwing all my clothes on the floor again this morning. He had a lot to make amends for. Thank god, the people he cared most about were willing to give him a second chance, even if it was rough to earn back their trust.

They climbed in silence. Chace's muscles burned from exertion, his head aching from dehydration. He'd thought to bring canteens but not place them where he could reach them easily. The result: he wasn't about to fall a few thousand feet to his death to grab a sip of water.

Spotting a break in the rocky ascent, he maneuvered his body slowly towards the cave. They both needed a brief rest after their ten hours scaling this peak, and he was too thirsty not to stop for water.

"I am ... so sick ... of climbing mountains," he breathed, hauling himself over the edge of a shallow, tall cave big enough for him and Gunner.

"*You* hate it?" Gunner grunted in return, his head popping up over the edge. "What about me?"

I need to fly again. Chace tugged free a couple of protein bars. He waited until Gunner had settled on the other side before tossing one to him. They ate quietly and caught their breath. Chace's attention went to the sky outside the small cave.

"You sure about this?" he asked.

"I wouldn't be climbing a damn mountain if not," came the panther shifter's disgruntled response.

"You can sense her. Why can't I?" Chace grumbled. It was more than his frustration about his stymied magic. It was the knowledge that the shifters were able to sense Skylar – and he wasn't. He was cut off from her completely, despite the cabin using magic to bring them to the foothills of the mountains where Gunner's shifter GPS told them to go.

"Something will work out," Gunner said. "It has to at this point. You were too powerful, and Gavin is gone. My magic returned soon after."

Chace said nothing, knowing his magic wasn't responding for a different reason. He had to *earn* it back after callously giving it up. The cabin had returned, but he was still unable to reach the shifter fire locked deep within him. One of the women in his life had forgiven him. The other hadn't yet.

What would it take? Watching everyone he cared about die?

"How much farther do you think it is?" he asked restlessly.

"Not far. Feels like she's right on top of us."

The bellow from some large creature bounced around the mountains. Chace and Gunner froze, the panther shifter tilting his head.

"Smells like a cat," Gunner said. "Big one. Lion."

"As long as it's not a griffin," Chace said. He leaned out of the cave and looked up. The sound had come from an unseen ledge near the peak of the mountain they were scaling. "Is that where we're headed?"

"Yep."

Chace considered how big the creature was that made such a sound then shrugged. "You can speak cat. We'll be fine."

Gunner said nothing.

After a few more minutes, they replaced their packs and began the last part of their ten-hour ascension.

Chace went first, gripping handholds with tired fingers. He felt himself fall into the zone, the rhythm of his movement calming his thoughts. Hand, foot, foot, hand. The grey rock before his eyes was streaked with white, black and peach, and he followed the crisscrossing veins of color with some interest.

Gunner was quiet as he climbed a few feet away, the two of them connected by a thick blue rope.

I have no idea what I did to deserve a friend like this. Chace thought, aware of how much felines hated heights and mountains.

A shadow crossed over them.

"Think we got company," Gunner said quietly.

Chace looked from the rock wall to the sky above. With his precarious balance, he wasn't able to lean back enough to see what it was. "Can't see it. Can you smell what it is?"

"Feathers," Gunner growled.

"You gotta be more specific."

Another shadow fell over them. A second roar followed it from the great cat on the peak above.

Chace balanced himself and risked bending back farther than usual to get a good look at the sky.

"Shit," he muttered. "Griffins. Small ones, though. Not Dillon."

"They can sense your girl like I can."

"What the hell is she doing up here? I have to assume the cat is Mason."

"No way he came up here voluntarily."

Chace frowned and quickened his climb as much as he dared, uncertain what it meant that Mason and Skylar were stuck on a ledge at the top of a mountain. How did they get there and more importantly, *why?*

The griffins were circling the peak, unconcerned with the two humans scaling the cliff wall. The lion above gave out an occasional roar of warning, while Chace worked on moving faster.

When he was a couple of meters from the ledge, he glanced up and looked back.

The massive head of a black lioness was hanging over the edge, her shoulders hunkered and massive paws gripping the edge. Her piercing stare was a beautiful, familiar blue.

"Um, Gun?" Chace called. "Is this an issue?"

The lion's ears flickered back then forward again, and she gave a throaty growl.

"Friendly," Gunner said. "Cats don't purr when they want to kick your ass."

"You sure that's a purr?"

"Yeah."

The cat disappeared, and seconds later, he heard her roar again. One of the griffins had ventured close to the peak and flew away quickly at the lion's warning.

Chace continued to climb, not convinced the lioness was welcoming them to the peak. He reached the top and pulled himself up.

A huge black claw swiped at him, snagging his backpack and yanking him onto the ledge. Before he could react, she'd pulled the backpack free and tossed it. The lioness pounced on it, leaving Chace alone.

What the hell? He rose, unable to take his eyes off the beast.

He'd never seen any feline this size – even Mason. Bigger than a Clydesdale with a powerful, lean body, the lioness's claws were longer than his fingers and her paws the size of his head.

"She's hungry," Mason said from behind him.

Chace turned.

Mason was smiling. He nodded towards the edge, and Chace glanced over to see Gunner's hands appearing over it. He strode to his friend and offered his hand. Gunner took it, and Chace hauled him over the edge.

The lioness was trying unsuccessfully to open the backpack. She gripped it with her paws then tried to bite it open, only for the backpack to slide through her paws. With a frustrated yowl, she grabbed it with powerful jaws and flung it towards Mason.

"Is she uh … clumsy?" Gunner asked.

"Not clumsy." Mason knelt beside the backpack. He unzipped it and grabbed a few protein bars. "She can take on the shape but has to learn the motor skills, like a cub."

Chace watched, not realizing the silent feline had crept up to him until her hot breath was on the back of his neck. He went rigid, uncertain what to think of the massive cat.

She nudged him, the simple move enough to push him a few steps.

"Remember what I told you? Gently," Mason warned. "No claws."

"Why is she staring at me?" Chace asked, not wanting to imagine what those claws would do to him. He'd spent enough time almost dying on the beach to know he didn't want anything to do with being shredded by a she-cat.

The lioness pawed the air between them with a growl.

"You can try it," Mason answered the question only he understood. "Gently."

One moment Chace was on his feet facing the great beast. The next, she'd wrapped her front two legs around him and threw him to the ground then sat on him.

Stunned, he wasn't able to move beneath the weight of the lion.

With a playful nip in the air, she planted her paws on either side of his head and licked him from neck to the top of his forehead.

"Omigod!" he said with a grunt, grimacing at the feel of her rough tongue. "This is so gross!"

"Aww, she likes you!" Gunner said.

"Here, Sky." Mason called. "Food."

The lioness launched off him and trotted to Mason, who dangled the protein bars he'd unwrapped in the space in front of him.

"Did you say Sky?" Chace demanded, sitting. He wiped the spit off his face.

Mason tossed protein bars into the air. Chace watched the lioness leap a good five meters into the air to catch them.

"In related news, we figured out what her power is as a Protector," Mason said. "She can use the magic of the nearest shifter to change into something big enough to kick that shifter's ass."

Chace stared at him, digesting the words slowly. He looked again at the lioness, and he suddenly understood why her blue eyes were so familiar. Exchanging a look with Gunner, he approached the great cat.

"Sky?" he asked doubtfully.

She faced him, ears flickering back and forth.

"We've been up here since last night," Mason said with a sigh. He dug out the canteen from Chace's backpack. "I think she got tired of shifting. We were practicing but didn't expect to get stuck here or for *them* to show up." He motioned to the sky.

Skylar's ears flattened back, and she bared her teeth at the griffins.

"Or maybe she's living up to her role and protecting you," Chace suggested. "So you're saying she can shift into anything?"

"We think so."

"If I'm here, can she turn into a panther?" Gunner asked.

Skylar's attention rested on them again. She looked curiously at Gunner then closed her eyes.

"I can't believe it's her," Chace said in a hushed voice. "Are you sure?"

"Definitely," Mason replied.

"How'd you get up here?"

Mason's features became shuttered. He didn't respond.

Damn cats.

Skylar growled. Chace stepped away from her, recognizing the tremor of magic in the air that indicated she was getting ready to shift. She stretched out on her belly. Her body began to change and the skin beneath her fur ripple. Her thick fur turned from black to brown to tawny while her head grew narrower and her nose elongated. Her size shrank and her body grew lankier, leaner, until she resembled a large panther rather than a lion.

When finished, she let out a long, pain-filled grumble then lay still for a moment.

"Holy shit," Chace murmured, kneeling beside her. He rested a hand on her head. "You really are a shifter queen." A smile spread across his face, and he petted her ears then trailed his fingers down her long snout.

She was gazing at him steadily. Her tail flickered, and she twisted.

"No, Sky," Mason said.

"What's wrong?" Chace asked, confused.

Skylar sat then stood and began chasing her tail.

"I remember that," Gunner said with a loud laugh. "When you first learn to shift, your tail really just ... drives you crazy. It has a mind of its own."

Chace watched Skylar chase her tail in circles for a moment.

Abruptly, she leapt into the air, surpassing Gunner's ten-foot vertical, a large paw with claws extended.

She tagged a griffin's wing. It gave squawk of pain before staggering away into the sky. Feathers floated to the ground, and she sat, tail flickering behind her as she glared up at the two circling griffins.

"Can you change into something that can fly?" Gunner asked Skylar.

She leveled a look at Chace.

"Don't look at me," he half-joked. "I got nothing. Can you shift into a human?"

Skylar hunkered down to the ground. Her growl turned softer, and she closed her eyes once again.

"Clothes." Mason tossed a folded set to Chace then turned around.

Chace set them down beside her. He almost didn't turn away, wanting to see every inch of her gorgeous golden skin, then decided not to mess with a panther. He turned away as well, listening to the sounds of her body breaking a part to reform itself. A thrill went through him at the idea she was one of them, along with the sense of amazement that she could shift into *anything*. If Mason were right about her turning into a bigger version of any shifter, how large of a dragon would she become around him?

If I could get my magic back. He clenched his teeth together, once again plagued by the doubt he'd felt the past few days. *What if it never returns?*

The sounds of a shifter changing shape ceased, and he heard the brush of clothing against skin as Skylar got dressed. It took every ounce of his will power not to turn around, knowing her naked skin was so close to him.

"More griffins," Mason said, eyes on the sky.

"I almost got one," Sky said. "I need more protein bars."

Chace faced her to find her gazing up at him. She looked exhausted from shifting, but her blue eyes shone brightly.

41

"Hey," she murmured.

"Hey." He resisted the urge to take her into his arms, to feel her skin and know she was safe and well.

"I couldn't feel your magic," she said, disappointed. "The cabin came back without it?"

"Looks that way."

She was studying him. He felt a familiar jolt of desire stir his blood. He was almost close enough to smell her peachy shampoo.

Skylar caught the bars Mason tossed her.

"So ... after all the complaining you've done about shifters ..." Chace started, unable to contain his amusement.

"Our roles are reversed," she snapped.

"Ouch."

"Not to interrupt, but do you feel ready to shift again, Sky?" Mason asked. "We've got incoming."

She rubbed her face with one hand, clearly tired.

"You gonna tell us how you got up here?" Chace asked her.

Her gaze shot up, and she narrowed her eyes. He didn't understand the sudden flare of anger that crossed his features.

"If I push you off the cliff, will you be able to fly?" she asked, folding her arms across her chest. She walked away from him to snatch the canteen from his backpack.

"What's going on?" Chace demanded.

"What's going on is that we need a way down from here," Mason said. "Quickly. I'm open to ideas."

"If we grab a griffin, maybe I can shift into one?" Skylar asked. "I couldn't quite feel them."

"You mean steal their magic?" Gunner asked.

"You felt it?" she asked curiously.

"Yeah."

Chace couldn't take his eyes off her. There were moments over the past few days where he hadn't thought he'd ever see her again. Now that she was before him, he wasn't entirely certain whether he was happy or frustrated.

"If you need a break, we can take over bird control," Gunner offered. "You up for it, Mason?"

"Yeah." Mason wolfed down a protein bar.

He and Gunner moved away to shift while Chace turned his gaze overhead. The two griffins had been joined by three more, all much smaller than Dillon.

But it was just a matter of time before their leader sought them out.

Skylar joined him, eating her bars quickly and quietly. She tucked the last wrapper in her pocket. Too aware of everything she did, of her body heat and scent, Chace struggled not to break the plane between them. He still didn't know where they stood, especially after their interaction when her father was killed.

"I can't feel your magic, Chace," she murmured, breaking the awkward silence between them. "But ... it's there, isn't it? You healed me, and the cabin came back to life."

"It's somewhere," he agreed.

By her long look, she was thinking. Hard. He wasn't able to read her.

"How's it feel to be one of us?" he asked.

"Shifting hurts."

"You get used to it."

Still the look.

Chace wasn't able to interpret it. Unable to stand so close without touching her, he took her cool hand.

Her expression softened, and she glanced down at their clasped hands.

"I keep thinking I don't know why my mother wasn't able to shift and protect herself," she said.

He wasn't certain what to say, so he kept quiet.

"I wonder if her magic was trapped like yours," she added. "Because it's in you, isn't it?"

"Every once in a while I feel it," he said.

"When you're with me?"

"Usually when you're in danger. Like with Dillon, or when I healed you."

"Except for Gavin." Her hushed tone and averted gaze made him realize how much she was hurting.

"That I can't explain, except maybe because he was there, the magic figured he'd save you." He squeezed her hand.

"Interesting. So maybe, if I'm in danger and only you can save me …"

"I don't know," he said. "You know how moody dragons and their magic can be. I'm working on myself, but I can't begin to guess how much I have to make up for."

She was studying him again. "You've changed a little, haven't you?"

"A lot, I'd say." He smiled. "Still wanna drag you off and fuck you."

Red crept up her neck and face.

"Or … maybe that was too much, too fast."

"No, it's okay," she murmured.

The roar of Mason made them both turn. He'd succeeded in dragging one griffin out of the air. As they watched, he tore out its throat then tossed the carcass over the ledge. There were six more griffins in the sky, and two of them were huge.

"If they start working together to corner our cats, we won't last long," Chace observed. He went to the ledge and peered over. Skylar kept a hold of his hand and moved with him. "There's no fast way down that would save us from getting killed if we tried."

"We don't have much time to figure this out."

"Shit," he muttered. There were twice as many in the skies, and they'd started to coordinate their attacks on the great cats. "Sky, get down!" He pushed her to the ground and covered her with his body.

A griffin slashed his back. Chace grated his teeth together, aware of the warm body beneath his.

The creature flew off, and Chace rolled.

Another was diving for them.

He yanked Skylar up and towards the rocky peak at one end of the ledge. Ducking between the boulders and rock wall, they barely escaped the long talons of the griffin pursuing them. It swept up and away.

"I think we have a problem," he said, eyeing the other griffins.

"We could really use a dragon right about now," Skylar said in frustration.

"I know, Sky." Her words stung more than he wanted her to know. "If I knew how to make it work …" He shook his head.

"I have an idea."

He glanced at her. Her eyes were on the sky.

"It's not a pretty one," she added with a half-smile. "And if it works, you have to swear now that you'll forgive me."

He almost asked what she had planned but stopped himself, deciding that he not only trusted her, but meant he'd do whatever it took to win her over. "Whatever you have in mind, I'm all in?"

"Good. Do you think I can fly if I shift into a griffin?" she asked almost absently. "I can feel their magic."

"No way," he said firmly. "If you had trouble using your paws as a lioness, you're not going to know how to fly."

She frowned. "Okay then. Well, my idea –"

The dive of a griffin cut her off. She ducked down, and he mirrored her movement.

This griffin was smarter. He landed on the boulder in front of them and began slashing at them with one talon and his beak.

Chace tumbled out from the safe spot, Skylar landing on top of him. They vaulted to their feet and started to run. Not two steps later, he was yanked backwards as the griffin tore Skylar away from him.

"Chace!" Skylar's cry made his chest seize.

He spun in time to see a large griffin hauling her away. She was panicking and wriggling, trapped in long talons wrapped around her body.

"Sky!" he shouted. "Gunner!"

The big cat turned then darted towards them.

Chace chased after the beast. He didn't have a chance for the helplessness to steal his hope. One second he was running, the next, he, too, was being dragged into the midday sky. The talons around his midsection gripped him tightly, and his breath caught as he stared at the two cats on the peak below. They grew smaller quickly as the griffin charged into the sky.

Chace twisted to see what direction they went and was somewhat relieved to see that they were following the griffin that had Sky. He mentally calculated how long they'd have to wait for a dragon to find them.

At least six hours. Way too long. His frustration turned to fury, mostly directed at himself. His magic wasn't responding to him, even now, when they were in danger. Not one tiny spark filled his blood when he begged it to.

The griffins didn't take them far. Across one mountain range, over a lower range of peaks and onward to a towering plateau with sheer, rock walls pockmarked by caves. There was no visible way down except to fly.

The griffin lowered them to the ground then dropped him and landed, folding its wings.

Chace climbed to his feet, eyes seeking Skylar.

She was a few dozen feet away, separated from him by three large griffins.

"You okay?" he called.

"Yeah." She met his gaze. "You?"

He nodded. "About that idea of yours ..."

A griffin snapped at him.

Skylar appeared uncertain, as if she wasn't convinced her idea was going to work. She looked away.

"It's okay if it involves lassoing me or injecting me with fire," he said.

"Nothing like that," she assured him. "Something worse."

Not sure what that means.

"You promise you won't hate me, right?" she asked again.

"Never," he vowed quickly.

"We'll see." She smiled. "If it works, maybe we can figure out a way to start over. Together." Her face grew pink.

Despite the milling griffins, his gaze became riveted to her features. "I'd do anything for that chance with you, Sky."

"I'm counting on it."

"How touching." Dillon's sharp voice came from beyond the griffins. They parted to move out of his way, and he walked towards Skylar. "I didn't think you'd survive, Chace."

I really hate that man right about now. "I'm a lucky dragon."

"I'll make sure you die right this time." Dillon's dark eyes slid to Skylar and lingered.

"We're both here. What's your grand plan, griffin?" Chace asked, wanting to keep Dillon's attention off Sky.

"Simple. Kill you and use her to find my enemies while they sleep. Easy way to end a war."

"What war, Dillon?" Skylar demanded. "One you started because of what happened to your father?"

"You leave him out of this!" Dillon snarled. His face turned red while his eyes flashed with anger. "You had to kill him, didn't you, Sky?"

"For the zillionth time, no! Mason did. Your own ally killed him."

Dillon rolled his eyes. "Former ally. Nonetheless Mason wouldn't do such a thing."

Chace heard Skylar make a growling sound. He resisted the urge to move closer to her when Dillon paused in front of her. Every instinct in his body screamed for him to protect her, but he wasn't about to make matters worse around the lunatic when he had no way to help them out of this situation.

"Chill, Sky," he said softly.

She glanced at him and took a deep breath.

"The griffins tell me you can shift into a panther, and I'm able to sense you, which means your power has awoken," Dillon said, circling her. "I can't imagine how being a panther is very beneficial.

What else can you do, if anything?"

"No idea," she snapped. "Seeing as how you brainwashed me to try to control the shifters, I've got no knowledge whatsoever about what I'm supposed to do."

"There's more. I know it," Dillon insisted. "How can you turn into a panther? *Why* a panther? How can that be the great gift that allows you to control the shifters?"

Chace listened, realizing Dillon had no idea what Skylar was capable of. He inched closer, earning him a glare and gnashing of teeth from the nearest griffin. Infuriated by his helplessness, he stopped and thought hard.

"It's not about control, Dillon," Skylar replied. "It's about protecting them from things like this – wars, other shifters trying to kill them. From things like *you*."

"I'm not the problem. This war has been going on for thousands of years. The griffins may have been hiding quietly for some time, but it never truly ended," he returned. "That dragon whore gave us a means to continue it. She wanted what I want: to change the leadership of the shifters from birthright to the strongest. How else can we survive, if we are hiding from humans? The shifters need a leader who will keep order and discipline."

"And you propose doing that by killing off those who don't agree?" Chace challenged. "The leadership is by birthright because it takes the strongest of our kind to safeguard the shifters."

"Strong like *you*?" Dillon laughed bitterly. He approached Chace slowly, his eyes gleaming with satisfaction. "The great teal dragon, protector of the shifters. Where's your strength now, dragon? You're the weakest here. You don't even belong among our kind anymore!"

"It takes more than brute force to lead, Dillon. If I've learned anything, it's that strength without thought will get you where I am now," Chace responded with what calm he was able to muster. He imagined transforming into the largest dragon he could and snapping Dillon in two.

"Weak," Dillon repeated. He lowered his voice to a whisper.

"Does it bother you that your woman and everyone else pities you? What use are you to anyone?"

Chace said nothing. He'd struggled with the same thoughts for days now. Unable to help Sky the way he was supposed to let alone the rest of the shifters, he had spent more hours than he wanted to admit lost in the confines of his mind, wondering why he was even alive when he had nothing to give.

Except I do. Aware of Skylar's gaze on him, he knew his place was with Sky. Somehow. If they didn't survive this together, if he didn't earn back his magic, the shifter community would be devastated by a war. There was a way to correct the course of events Dillon wanted for the shifters. Chace just had to recover his power and help Skylar make things right.

"Freyja always told me you were the strongest ever born. Stronger even than Gavin," Dillon added. "Like most things, that dragon bitch was wrong."

"Freyja?" Chace repeated. While at the cabin on the Oregon beaches, waiting to die, he'd dreamt about Freyja, the woman he'd one time loved and who made his dragon magic awaken originally. She'd claimed Dillon was too brutish to be the mastermind behind the slayer movement. "What about her?"

"She's the head of the slayers," Skylar said tersely. "She left Mason and me on the peak where you found us. She's behind the brainwashing and kidnapping of the shifters."

Chace stared at her, not expecting to hear the news about his ex.

"She wanted what I want: to rule the shifter community and to disable the ability for her enemies to defy her. Nearly all the griffins were put to sleep," Dillon added. "Then the dragons that opposed her."

She's strong enough to talk to people even when she was put to sleep. He doubted she'd gotten much traction, though, if Dillon hadn't had his own reason for wanting to help her.

"So you helped Freyja get rid of anyone who might oppose her and brainwash the one person who could someone keep power over the shifters. Then you probably planned to kill me to ensure I never helped Skylar wake up from what you did," Chace said thoughtfully. "I imagine you'll have to knock Freyja off when the work is done and you no longer need her help."

"More or less. This way works, too," Dillon added. "It ends soon." He spun away and motioned for a few griffins to take flight. "I'll let her know we have you, Chace, and see if that flushes her out of sleep mode. If not, I'll torture you in front of Skylar until she tells me where to find the dragons."

Chace shared a long look with Skylar. By the fear in her gaze, she knew he was defenseless and they were both fucked.

Dillon headed towards the edge of the plateau.

"Dillon, wait!" she called. "Mason said you know what happened to my mother."

"Do what I tell you, Sky, and I might tell you what I did to her and how long she screamed. I might even wait to torture Chace for a day or two." Dillon didn't bother looking at her. He spread his arms and jumped off the side of the plateau.

Seconds later, the massive griffin rose into the sky. He was trailed by several others while three remained to keep watch.

Skylar was watching him fly, pain in her beautiful blue eyes.

He hated that look, the one that silently asked him why he was broken. It made his heart ache and his gut twist. Not caring if the guard griffins snapped his arm off, Chace crossed to her. He instinctively took her in his arms, wanting to comfort her as much as he needed to feel her against him.

She clung to him for a moment, a tremor working through her warm frame. He squeezed her to him more tightly and nuzzled her hair.

"He's fucking with you," he said gently.

"Is he?"

Probably not. Chace held her, wishing he could take away her pain or at least, protect her from the danger headed their way. The familiar tension between them was more than sexual; there was pain and disappointment as well, emotions he felt both responsible for and powerless to remove. Was it selfish to want her to smile at him the way she had before their entangled lives got so complicated?

"I don't think there's any chance Ginger is alive," she murmured. "But I need to know what happened."

"I understand, honey. Now may not be the right time to figure it out," he advised with a glance at the griffins. They looked hungry. The moment Dillon no longer needed either of them alive, they'd be snapped in two. Skylar was going to be able to fly or hold her own for long if she shifted into a griffin. *If we get out of here, I swear I'll teach her to fly.* Even without his magic, he could mentor her well enough with a thousand years of knowledge.

She looked up at him. "You think we're in trouble?"

"I do. The dragons won't be flying until nightfall. We've got half a day to survive and are at Dillon's mercy." He considered the area where the griffins had imprisoned them. Sheer, rocky descents extended down every side of the plateau. "I'm not seeing any way off this rock."

"I have a better chance of killing griffins up here as a lion," she pointed out. "Or as a dragon."

Chace released her, hating himself for knowing he should have power he didn't. "Is this an I-told-you-so moment?"

"No, Chace," she said, taking his arm. "This is a I-hope-you're-serious moment. As in, I really hope you'd do anything to save me."

But I can't! He wanted to scream the words. Before he could remind her of his inadequacy, she took his cheeks in her hands and pulled his head down. Her kiss was deep and passionate, her warm lips claiming his with need he felt every time he saw her. His arms circled her instinctively, and he hauled her against his body. She tasted of the peanut butter protein bar she'd eaten before the griffins attacked, her velvety mouth his to explore while her hot tongue teased and tasted him.

He'd missed the feel of her body pressed against his, the firm breasts and feminine shape. One hand slid down to squeeze her ass, and he pressed his hardening erection against her lower belly, wanting more than anything for a few minutes alone with her to strip her clothes off and make love to her until they both slaked the hot desire torturing him.

Until she smiles again. God, he missed her contagious grin. There was so much sadness in her face now.

The squawk of a griffin jarred him, reminded him of where they were and how little they could afford to ignore their dangerous situation.

As if sensing the same, Skylar pulled away from their kiss, her breathing off and her sky-colored eyes riveted to his. She wound the fingers of one hand in his hair.

"Did you mean what you said the day Gavin died?" she whispered, searching his gaze.

He didn't want to think of everything he'd admitted that day. It was the painful moment when he realized the truth about himself, about how he'd never be good enough for the woman in his arms.

"Yes," he replied just as quietly. "I did. You are my other half. Even if you hate me forever, you are my heart."

Skylar smiled. "I hope that's enough."

His brow furrowed. The way she said it made him think she was referring to something other than their tangled up relationship. Before he could ask what she was talking about, she spoke again.

"We need to help the others." She planted her hands on his chest and pushed away lightly.

He released her. "You going to shift into a lion?" he asked. "Can you do that without Mason around?

"I don't think so. I need to test what I can do. But I can shift into something, hopefully." She glanced at the pacing griffins. "Are you ready for my plan?"

"Which is ...?"

"I told you before. If you mean what you say, you'll be ready to save me this time around," she said. "God help us both, if you're not. I'm gonna take a leap of faith that you'll be there for me."

Skylar followed the movement of the nearest griffin with her gaze then stealthily moved past him. Chace watched, the reality of what she was doing not clicking until he saw her pace quicken.

She was headed towards the edge of the plateau with a look of determination on her features that said she wasn't going to stop.

Leap of faith. Her intention slammed into him. Terror shot through him.

"Skylar, no!" he shouted and darted forward to grab her.

She ran off the cliff.

His hand grasped nothing but air, and he dropped to his knees and leaned over the edge, his emotions tumbling and whirling within him.

His Sky, the other half of his heart, the woman he loved, had jumped. His surroundings grew surreal, the sun too bright, the sight of her falling like watching a slow motion film. Emotions blazed through him, and he experienced the panic he felt the last time he'd seen her fall, when Gavin was there to catch her.

This time, there was no one but him who could save her.

"*No!*" he roared.

A trickle of warmth hit his blood stream.

I won't let you die, Sky! Their fates were intertwined; their hearts beat as one. If hers stopped, so would his.

Chace jumped, no longer caring what happened to him. He didn't want to be in a world without his heart.

Chapter Six

SKYLAR RECALLED TOO WELL the first time she fell out of the sky: The rush of air, the way her eyes watered until everything below her became a splotchy blur of colors. She was falling fast enough that she could barely breathe and yet, she felt like she'd never hit the ground, because her mind and senses seemed to slow. She was stuck between panic and hope, between despair and the instinct that made her jump in the first place.

Without Chace's magic, they weren't going to make it off the plateau or survive long enough for the dragons to find her. She definitely thought jumping off a mountain beat seeing Chace and his ex together.

Maybe I'm being stupid about this. The thought would've made her laugh in borderline hysteria, if she'd been able to catch her breath enough to laugh. *Or maybe I'm wrong and I'm about to splatter on the rocks below.*

The grey boulders that looked like pebbles from above were getting larger, closer, and sorrow replaced her hope. What if she was wrong? What if Chace's magic really wasn't coming back, and she was the last hope the others had of standing some chance against Dillon and Freyja?

The ground was getting closer.

Emotions bubbled within her. Regret, sadness ...

Anger.

Was this all there really was? A life full of stolen memories and people who betrayed her?

The thought of never seeing Chace again was worse than the idea of smashing into the boulders. Of everyone who walked away from her, he'd at least come back and owned up to the truth: he was broken, but he was willing to do what he could to make things right. She had a ton of unfinished business in her life, but there was only one thing she regretted doing in the last few seconds of her life – not taking a second chance on Chace.

No matter how angry she was with him, he'd long since stolen her heart.

Aware her time was almost up, Skylar closed her eyes and prepared herself to die, willing their bond to carry her farewell message to him.

You're my dragon, Chace. You fucked up, but so did I. I forgive you for hurting me. I'm just sorry that we'll never get our pizza date.

And then she released what she suspected was her final breath.

A familiar, burning sensation went through her a moment before she was snatched out of the air. Skylar gasped at the sudden change in direction. She went from falling fast to soaring away from the boulders at a speed that made her neck snap and darkness creep into her mind.

She blinked rapidly and saw how close she'd come to the ground. Disoriented by the sudden movement, she struggled to keep from falling unconscious at the speed with which she was climbing into the sky.

Skylar twisted. Though her vision was blurry, there was no mistaking the teal shade of Chace's wings as they beat the air around them, compelling them up the cliff towards the heavens.

He flew away from the plateau where they'd meet Dillon, back towards the peak where Mason and Gunner still fought off half a dozen griffins. Chace deposited her on the ledge close to the great cats then soared into the sky overhead.

Skylar trembled from the horrible adventure and struggled to shake the darkness out of her head. She sat back on her haunches, too unsteady to risk rising. Her gaze followed the massive teal dragon into the sky with no short amount of awe.

She'd never been able to look at Chace in his dragon form without being stunned by his size and beauty. His long wings took him quickly towards the griffins. Within seconds, he was belching fire at one, charring its wings enough that it plummeted to the ground. He tucked his wings and charged at another, his forearm-long fangs snapping its neck in midair, before it had a chance to flee.

He shredded the wings of another griffin with his talons then slung one down to the two felines to take care of before taking off at top speed to deal with the two griffins that decided to flee.

Skylar watched his displays of incredible strength and agility, mesmerized by the creature's beauty and fearlessness. It took a moment for the fog to clear from her mind enough for her to realize how right she'd been.

With nothing but himself in the way, Chace had to make a choice. Either he loved her enough to save her, no matter what the cost, or he wasn't capable of overcoming his pride - ever.

He really does love me. Tears filled her eyes. She swiped them away and climbed to her feet.

"Now, I will definitely tell you I-told-you-so, you fire-breathing bastard," she murmured to him. *I knew you could do it. You just needed to trust yourself.*

Mason and Gunner were watching as well, the two felines standing shoulder-to-shoulder with their tails flicking. She joined them.

"Looks like he's fixed," she observed with a shaky laugh. "Probably pretty pissed, too." *Which he deserves.*

Mason turned his large head towards her. Red blood contrasted with the black fur around his mouth. He shook his head then padded away. A few seconds later, she heard him shifting.

Gunner seemed content to stay in his feline shape. He sat and continued to gaze at the sky warily, mouth open in a light pant.

"What the hell happened?" Mason asked when he'd shifted. Wearing his jeans, he pulled on his t-shirt as he approached. "One minute we were batting griffins out of the sky. The next, you two were gone, and then he just appears."

"Yeah." She smiled. A sense of pride went through her, as much from knowing she'd pegged Chace correctly as it was from marveling at how beautiful he was in the sky, now that he was back.

Finished chasing the griffins, Chace appeared to be reveling in his first experience flying in weeks. He soared and rolled, shot up so high into the sky that she could barely see him then plummeted close enough to the mountains that it didn't seem possible for him to stop. He spit fire and bellowed a few times, and played with an air current, hovering in place and tipping his wings back and forth to test where the wind would take him.

"My god he's beautiful!" she breathed. She could almost feel his joy. It was as powerful as his sorrow had been, the part of him that was missing now fully restored. "I wonder if I can change into a dragon now." She sought out the magic.

It was strong and warm, humming through her body. She hadn't realized how much she missed the thrum of his energy. At one time, it had been overwhelming and annoying, a connection to a creature she had thought of as her enemy. Now, it was so much more: a bond she craved to a dragon that had just proven to be the man she prayed he could be.

"No." Mason rested a hand on her arm. "You may be able to shift, but you still have to learn things when you do. There's no way you can fly the first time out."

"Ugh. True." She eyed the cliff's edge, unwilling to take a tumble out of the sky again. If she shifted into a dragon bigger than Chace, he'd be unable to save her this time, either.

"We have to get off this cliff. I need a shower, and I could eat a damn deer." Mason grated. He stepped away and began waving his arms to get Chace's attention.

Unable to help herself, Skylar simply grinned, eyes on the dragon circling above them.

Will I be a pink dragon? She wondered.

Chace drifted down from the sky and landed at the other end of the ledge. He folded his wings, his dark blue depths settling on her. He snorted and stayed put.

She sensed he was probably mad at her. At least, she'd be pissed if someone she loved jumped off a ledge to prove a point. Even if that point was how much he loved her.

Beaming a smile at him, she called out, "Let's get off this mountain, dragon!"

Chace's eyes narrowed, and his ears flattened back against his head. She heard his growl from her spot across the peak.

Skylar laughed.

"He doesn't sound happy," Mason observed.

"I really don't care," she said. "I won this round, and it was worth it."

Chace unfolded his wings and lifted himself into the air above them.

Gunner gave a plaintive cry in his panther form, and Mason grimaced. Skylar, however, was eager to get off the mountain, even if it was by dragon.

With gentleness that conveyed none of his anger, Chace picked them all up, one by one, and then began a gradual descent to the ground. Skylar watched the ground become closer, fascinated by the amount of strength it took for him to fly with such control and steadiness.

Mason was right. It had been difficult for her to gauge her strength as a lioness let alone curb it so she didn't hurt someone. How much harder was it going to be to do similar as a dragon? To *fly*? How did one learn in the first place?

Chace's magic was like a bonfire in her veins. It meant that she was able to turn into a dragon as well, now that his magic was freed.

She had a feeling being a dragon was much more complex than being a feline but couldn't wait to try it.

He took them to a picnic area at the base of the mountains and hovered in a meadow capable of accommodating his sixty-foot wingspan. Releasing them all a few feet from the ground, he then landed a short distance from them.

"We're about three kilometers from the compound," Mason assessed. "You all are welcome to return."

"Maybe," Skylar said and folded her arms across her chest. "I have a few things to say to your boss."

Mason averted his gaze in a sign that made her stomach sink. They both watched Gunner running across the field. He dropped his shoulder and rolled, grunting as he wriggled in the grass.

"Think he's happy to be back on solid ground," Mason said with a laugh. "I feel like doing the same thing."

Skylar's smile faded.

Mason glanced at her. "I should go. Freyja will be suspicious if I'm gone too long."

"If you're serious about being on the winning side, why don't you stay with us?" Skylar asked.

He considered her briefly before answering. "I've gotta take care of a few things."

"Now that I know what I can do, I'm putting as many of your people to sleep as I can," she added. "No more instigating this war between shifters. And your boss – she's got a ton of shit headed her way."

"I know." He studied her. "There are some people who deserve to know what we've done to them. Give me a day, Skylar, before you hunt us down. Enjoy your time with Chace, and let me break the news to those who don't yet know they've been brainwashed. I'm going to tear down the organization Freyja built from the inside out."

Skylar's anger with his involvement in the conspiracy of Dillon and Freyja softened. She believed him to be genuine. It was in the sorrow and regret she read in his eyes.

"I can't imagine how they will react," she said. "You don't have to do it alone, Mason."

"I need to," he said firmly. "I'm making amends the only way I know how. I can't change what I've done, but I can change what happens next. You're right, Sky. They deserve to know and to be given a choice."

Pitying him, she nodded. She heard the rustling of grass behind her as Chace made his way across the field.

Mason turned and began walking towards the forest.

Skylar hesitated. "Mason."

He turned.

"Thank you for doing this," she told him. "Really. I know how hard it will be."

He nodded. Without speaking, he turned away and disappeared into the forest.

Skylar watched him. She wanted to go with him, to try to help console those who were about to learn what she had the past few weeks.

Let him have his second chance, she told herself. Chace had been given his and succeeded in recovering what he'd lost. Mason would, too. Tomorrow morning, she'd seek him out again to make sure he'd followed through, then put those who insisted on following Freyja and Dillon into hibernation.

But Mason deserved the chance to right the wrongs he committed.

Chace's warm breath puffed down on her from above. Skylar craned her neck back to see his massive head hovering over hers, his sharp gaze lingering in the direction where Mason had gone.

Gunner got up and shook himself off then issued a mewling sound.

As if understanding what the panther shifter said, Chace responded with a quiet, rumbling growl.

Gunner loped away into the woods.

Skylar faced Chace. He glanced at her then leapt upward into the sky, as if he wasn't done reveling in his newfound freedom.

Or he's too pissed to turn into a human right now.

She shook her head, nonetheless proud. Her smile grew as she took in what remained in the meadow after he left it.

"Cabin!" she exclaimed, trotting forward.

The lights went on, and all the windows and door open in welcome.

Skylar hurried inside, anxious to be in the one place where she'd always felt safe and happy. The cabin was as she remembered it: welcoming, cozy and humming with subtle magic. The door and windows closed when she entered.

"How's life, cabin?" she asked, fingertips tracing down the back of the couch.

It didn't answer.

"How pissed is your dragon?"

A stack of books was shoved onto the floor.

"I thought so." Skylar sighed. Knowing he was mad did nothing to temper her happiness. She'd learned something far more important this afternoon.

Her eyes went to the bed where she'd first made love with Chace. She stood beside it, exhausted after her shifting exercises with Mason and the stress of being stuck on a peak for almost an entire day without decent food or water. Skylar slung herself across the bed and groaned.

It was still the most comfortable place she'd ever slept in her life. Maybe it was the magic cabin or maybe it was just being able to lay down somewhere without worrying about dragons or griffins coming to get her, but she felt calm and centered after her swan dive off a mountain.

The only thing that would make her life complete in that moment: a dragon shifter who wasn't too furious to turn human.

She grinned, not caring how upset he was at the moment.

"I know just how to cheer you up, dragon," she murmured. "Hey, cabin. You got any sexy lingerie around?"

She waited a moment then pushed herself up to look around. At the bottom of the bed was exactly what she needed.

Chapter Seven

CHACE DIDN'T EXPECT IT to take him until nightfall to cool down. Not that he was in a hurry to give Skylar a piece of his mind, especially since he was able to fly again.

But, well, he kinda was. Every time he felt calm enough to shift back into his human form, the thought of what she'd done sent dragon fury pumping through him once more, sabotaging his attempt to shift.

So he soared up and around, unable to recall when flying had felt this good or when the world below had been so beautiful. Nothing was new about the familiar scenery or the way the wind tickled his sensitive muzzle and ears.

I'm different. He was surprised to realize just how much he'd changed. He had never noticed or appreciated how steady his wings were or how perfectly formed each and every pine tree below truly was. There was so much outside of himself he'd never been grateful for, including the damn slayer-turned-Protector who scared him shitless earlier in the day.

Landing in the field as twilight draped over the world, he willed himself to stay focused long enough to make it inside the cabin, whose lights glowed warmly, as if it was happy Skylar was there. The moment he touched her, he'd have no problems controlling his magic.

Assuming she *let* him touch her. If not, he'd be right back out in the field, unable to control his temper or his magic once more.

Chace shuddered and shifted back into his human form. Standing naked in the field, he took a deep breath and waited a moment to make certain he was calm enough not to start changing into his dragon shape involuntarily.

"Calm, calm. The most beautiful girl in the world is waiting for you. Just because she fucking threw herself off a cliff ..." The muscles beneath his skin rippled. He blew out a breath. "We're okay with that. We are ... okay. With. That."

The tension in his muscles eased.

The forest breeze skated across his bare skin, making him shiver. His gaze went to the cabin, and he started forward, his heart quickening at the idea of being near Skylar again.

Unwilling to think about how irked he'd be if she didn't want anything to do with him still, Chace opened the door of the cabin and stepped into his home.

Candles were lit in a couple of windows, creating a romantic, warm atmosphere. It smelled of incense – something slightly sweet.

Any thought he had about her not wanting anything to do with him banished when he saw her. Skylar wore a see-thru teddy, tied beneath her ample breasts and flowing down over a thong that left little to the imagination. She was lying on her belly, facing the door, as if waiting for him.

He froze.

"I see you're ready," she said with a laugh, gaze going hungrily down his naked body to his erection.

"Is this a trick?" he asked warily. "Is cabin messing with me, or are you going to disappear if I try to touch you?"

"Come and find out." Skylar rose, holding his gaze. She tossed her dark hair over one shoulder and moved towards him. Her large breasts were barely contained in the nighty, and her skin glowed in the candlelight.

Desire spun through Chace, mixed with both hope and sorrow. The last few times he'd made love to Skylar, he'd been convinced he'd lose her afterwards. Being with her was bittersweet, a reminder they were at the beginning of what might become a full-blown shifter war. One they may not both survive.

Chace reached out and rested a hand on her arm, tracing it lightly from shoulder to wrist. The other half of his heart stood before him, gazing up at him without the anger or hurt she'd expressed the last few times they'd been together.

"You are so beautiful," he whispered, cupping one cheek in his hand. He gazed deeply into her eyes and saw the tiny flame in her pupil. "I have no idea what I did to deserve someone like you, Sky." She was close enough for her body heat and faint scent to reach him.

Yet he feared touching her, feared that he wasn't yet worthy enough or worse, that she still might reject him after what he'd done.

"You'll always be my dragon, Chace." The softness of her voice, coupled with the unguarded warmth in her gaze, was his undoing.

Chace wrapped his arms around her and hugged her to him hard. Her body molded against his. He buried his face in her hair and breathed in her familiar scent. Its effect was immediate; tension fled his frame. As turned on as he was by the near naked body pressed to his, he needed a hug more to reassure him that she – and they – were real.

Wetness on his chest made him move away. "You okay?" he asked.

Skylar nodded. She was trembling.

"Sky, what's wrong?"

She was quiet for a moment then lifted her head to gaze at him. Tears sparkled in her eyes. "When I was falling, there was a moment I thought you weren't coming for me."

"You thought I didn't care enough."

She nodded.

"You know better now?"

She gave him a watery smile, and he marveled at it. It was free of the disappointment and pain she'd expressed the past two weeks.

His Sky was back in his arms, where she belonged.

"Baby, I'll always catch you from here on out," he said with a faint smile. He wasn't about to tell her that there had been a moment when falling where he, too, didn't know if they'd make it. "You're my heart."

"I know," she replied. "I'm sorry about the cliff."

"Not a problem." He forced himself to say.

She laughed, hearing the reluctance in his tone. Skylar took his face in her hands once more, rose up on her tiptoes and kissed him lightly before dropping back onto her flat feet.

"I want this to be my home and you and cabin to be my family," she murmured.

Chace was quiet. He'd never thought such simple words could affect him so easily or that he, too, might one day want his own family. His throat was too tight for him to respond, the intense warmth blooming in his chest making him ache for a reason other than because he was aroused.

"Is that okay?" There was a tremor in Skylar's voice at his silence.

Chace drew her against him once more, holding her warm frame tightly. "Yes, Sky," he managed at last. "That's more than okay."

She sighed.

He let a hand travel down her back to her perfect ass. Chace slipped a finger between the thong and her skin and ran it around her hip, pausing at her lower belly.

"I need you, Sky," he whispered.

She lifted her head, the fire of desire burning in her eyes as well. She tugged the ribbon holding her teddy in place free then shrugged it off her shoulders to expose the firm mounds of her breasts.

Chace kept one hand on her backside to press her against his aching erection. With his other, he released the thong and slid his hand up her torso, admiring the way the candlelight cast shadows along her feminine curves. Taking one breast in his hand, he teased the nipple with this thumb then lowered his head to kiss her.

Skylar was pliant in his arms, her arms circling his neck. Chace kissed her leisurely, savoring her flavor and the heat of her mouth. Her skin was so smooth and soft, her body fitting against his perfectly. He couldn't remember a moment that felt more real or a woman he wanted all the way to the depths of his soul.

She responded to him with the same deep hunger he was experiencing.

"Let me see that ass in a thong before I strip it off you," he whispered huskily, withdrawing.

She smiled and turned in his arms, wriggling her backside against his erection. Chace growled in satisfaction at the sight of the thin black rope that slid between her cheeks to the place he wanted to be.

"So sexy," he murmured. He tightened his grip around her, drawing her body fully against his once more. His dick settled against the firm, plush spheres of her ass, and he moved suggestively against her.

Skylar lifted her arms to wrap them back around his neck, exposing her body to him completely.

Chace nipped her neck then kissed a trail from her ear to her collarbone. His hands roamed her body, one cupping and twisting a tight nipple gently while the other palm slid down her body to the apex of her thighs.

"Yes," she whispered, head lolling back against his chest.

For his first night with the woman he chose to spend the rest of his life with, he wasn't about to rush it or fail to appreciate every small part of it.

Chace slid two fingers into the plump folds of her sex, past the swollen clit and to the slick heat of her core. He dipped them inside the tight sheathe to rub her G-spot, and Skylar groaned.

"I definitely could do this every night for the rest of our lives," he whispered.

She wiggled her butt and pressed it harder to his erection.

He pulled his fingers free of her depths then loosened his grip on her, kneeling to tug off the thong. She stepped out of it, and Chace twisted her hips to face him. He lifted one of her legs and draped it over his shoulder, eyes on his target – the pink nether lips of her sex.

Skylar wound her hands through his hair, gasping when his tongue teased her swollen clit. He licked her firmly then slid his tongue down to her core. Intoxicated by the scent and taste of her arousal, Chace closed his eyes to savor both, listening to her breathing grow irregular as he drank from her core and traced the sensitive path back to her clit. He circled it with his tongue a few times, gripping her ass with one hand to keep her pressed to his mouth.

She gave a throaty moan that pushed his control closer to slipping.

"I love the way you taste, Sky," he said, raising his head. "And my god … the way you smell …" He took her hips then kissed a trail from her nether lips to her lower belly. He pushed her gently back towards the bed, walking on his knees until her legs bumped the bed, and she sat.

Chace tugged her closer to the edge, positioning her. He lowered his mouth to her core once more, the urge to taste her sweet nectar inhuman. Her knees parted to give him access, and he buried his face in the sacred spot between her legs, breathing in the scent of her arousal then devouring her flavor with intensity driving his need. He slid two fingers into her once more, his tongue working in harmony with their movement to pleasure her.

Her hands ran through his hair and she pulled him into her body harder.

"Chace," her voice was as unsteady as her breathing. "I need to feel you inside me. Please!"

He continued for a moment, certain he'd never be able to satiate the yearning he had to drink from her. Her legs were quivering already in anticipation of the orgasm building, and he relented, wanting to be inside her when she came.

Straightening, Chace wrapped his arms around her and took one hard nipple in his mouth, circling, licking and grazing it with his teeth until she gasped. Her skin was warm against his, her body responding to his touch in a way that made him feel gratified, even before fucking her.

He kissed and nibbled her other nipple before lifting his face to hers. Skylar claimed his lips hungrily, her desire clear. Chace pushed her back onto the bed and settled between her thighs, determined to taste every last inch of her mouth before he let himself sink into her hot depths. Her skin was warm and soft beneath his, her plump breasts pressed to his chest and her fingernails trailing lightly down his back.

Had he ever thought it possible for every one of his senses to be so intoxicated by one woman? Her scent ensnared him, her sweet taste lingering in his mouth. He focused on the way her body moved beneath his, how lively and warm and soft she was.

What had he ever done to deserve someone so beautiful and sweet?

He left her mouth and spread hot kisses down her jaw. Her thighs were tight around his hips, her body trying to position itself to feel his dick at her core.

Chace gazed down at her, mesmerized by the glow on her cheeks and in her eyes. He brushed hair away from her face absently and held her gaze, unable to identify any other moment in his life that felt so intimate and powerful.

"Family," he murmured. The concept was so foreign – yet so right with her.

Skylar touched his face. She traced the line of his cheekbones then rested her warm palms on his cheeks.

"You'll always be my dragon," she said with a hint of a smile.

"You'll always be my heart." He gave a wicked half-smile and positioned his hips to penetrate her. He let the head of his arousal settle against her opening.

"Damn dragons," she whispered, the pinkish glow of her face growing darker.

He eased into her, inch-by-inch, relishing the heat and exquisite tightness of her sheathe while listening to her husky moan. He pushed himself deep into her and shuddered. He wasn't able to remember a time when simply entering a woman's body made him want to come.

Chace lowered his head beside hers and breathed in her scent, astonished by how good being inside her felt.

"We belong together," she said breathlessly. "Like this."

"Yeah." He gave an unsteady chuckle. Being inside her, pressing her to the bed, was far too natural. When his control was back, he met her gaze again. "I am so sorry for everything I did to hurt you."

"Show me." She smiled mischievously.

"Show you," he repeated. He moved in and out of her a few times with slow control, holding her gaze as he did so.

She groaned.

"I think I can do that," he said casually.

"Shut up!" She ordered in a breathless whisper and pulled his face down to hers.

Any thought he had of a long night of controlled passion melted under the intensity and demanding of her full lips. Dragon fire tore through him and into her, edging their desire higher, hotter than any he'd ever felt. Chace thrusted steadily but quickly, feeding the fire growing between them. He pressed himself the length of her body, needing to feel every inch of her against him, to capture every sigh and moan in his memory. His hands roamed her body in an attempt to satisfy the primal need to possess her fully, to brand every inch of her with his touch.

Skylar held nothing back, calling his name, arching, digging her nails into his ass ... She was uninhibited, responsive and intoxicating, a combination that left him pushing their passion farther, harder, closer to an explosive ending. Light sweat soon covered them both.

Chace rolled onto his back, his lips never leaving hers and his hips never still as he pumped faster and harder. She moved with him, her nails digging into his chest and shoulders, her hips riding his with building urgency.

"I never want this to end!" she gasped.

"It never has to," he responded.

Skylar smiled and closed her eyes, tossing her head back as the orgasm within her reached its peak.

Chace had never wanted to please anyone the way he did Sky, to feel her body respond to his touch and hear her cries when she climaxed. As many times as he'd touched her, it always felt like the first: magical, thrilling, and satisfying on a level that reached his soul. Everything from the flush of her cheeks to the wetness of her core was branded in his mind, an intangible treasure for him alone to safeguard. The dragon in him roared with triumph while the man wanted to weep in gratitude for being granted such an incredible gift as the woman in his bed, the other half of his heart.

They made love over and over, unable to satisfy the primal need to be one, to unite their bodies and magic with the powerful emotions stretching between them.

I'll never get enough of this woman. The thought stuck with him, even when sheer physical exhaustion forced them to take a breather some time later, curled in each other's arms. He breathed in their combined scents, more at peace than he'd ever experienced before. For the first time in his life, he not only knew where he belonged, but he'd found what made him happy. And he had a lifetime to experience every inch of her body over and over again.

Chapter Eight

AFTER THE FIREWORKS OF their long, sleepless night, Skylar should've been too exhausted to try to shift the next morning. If anything, she'd never felt so renewed, alive, or hopeful as she did standing across from the man who tenderly agreed to become the family she didn't have with emotion that left her feeling humbled and honored. Of all the people he'd met in a thousand years, the most incredible man in the world had chosen *her*.

The joy it caused was a source of amazing depths of energy, fed by the fire of his magic in her blood. She'd been unable to stop smiling like a lovesick fool. His honey-bonfire scent was ingrained on her skin and in her senses, saturating her with a smell that drove her wild yet left her feeling at peace as well.

"Where are you?" Chace's laugh drew her out of her blatantly adoring stare.

Skylar flushed. "Can't help it. I'm pretty happy right now."

Chace was eyeing her like he was ready to eat her or toss her back into bed, where they'd spent the night making love.

"Would you stop?" she asked with a playful laugh. "You're distracting me." Naked and exhilarated, she stood a few dozen feet from him in the field outside the cabin, trying hard to concentrate on shifting into a dragon instead of wanting to feel his skin against hers.

He crossed his arms, eyes lingering on her breasts. Chace wore a pair of sweats that rode low on his hips and nothing else, his chiseled features and muscular chest making her almost giddy with need and something deeper – the knowledge she had a home finally and a family.

Chace was her dragon. Forever.

Focus, Sky! She closed her eyes and internalized her senses, seeking out the strong flow of dragon magic that kept her from getting cold despite the chilly morning. She concentrated hard on the image of Chace in his dragon form then braced herself for the pain of shifting.

Agony and fire shot through her as her body broke, contorted, grew and reformed. The world fell away, and she surrendered to the pain, familiar fear going through her at the idea of what she was really doing: changing shapes. Turning into the creatures she used to hunt.

The pain diminished and disappeared when her body was done. Skylar lay still, trembling, exploring her new senses. She was able to smell every flower within miles and hear the soft hop of a rabbit making his way to food on the other side of the forest. The grass in the field tickled her nose, and the breeze ruffed her tufts of fur.

She cracked one eye open then the other, amazed at how far she was able to see. A glance at her wings told her she was a color of dragon between Chace's teal and Gavin's dark blue. Her talons appeared huge, her thick legs almost stubby. Her center of balance was much lower to the ground than when she'd been a cat, and her tail was heavier.

"Amazing," Chace said.

Skylar lifted her head to see him and tested her ears, making them flicker. When she stood up, her head would reach the top of the tree line around the meadow. She stayed hunkered down, with her belly on the ground, uncertain if she was ready yet to stand.

Chace approached and ran a hand down her side. Skylar shivered, not expecting her thick dragon hide to be so sensitive to touch.

"You're about my size," he said. "Looks like if we ever get in a spat, we better be human."

She snorted. Heat warmed her throat and mouth, and smoke spiraled out of her nostrils.

"Fire is like coughing. Just don't do it here. We can't set the forest on fire," he advised. He finished circling her and stood in front of her, gazing up at her with no short amount of satisfaction. "How do the wings feel?"

Skylar stood cautiously and then stretched them out on either side of her. They were light and thin enough to be translucent. She'd never thought of Chace's strong wings as being delicate, but they were, compared to the size and strength in the rest of her body.

"Flying is about balance and control. Your wings will always carry you, but you have to know when to adjust and when to let the wind guide you. It becomes instinctive after a while but can be a challenge at first."

They feel like tissue paper. She began to doubt her wings would hold her, even if they did stretch the length of the meadow.

"Give 'em a whirl," he instructed.

She eyed one doubtfully then lifted and lowered them. They didn't move straight up and down like she expected but at an angle. The simple movement lifted her a few inches off the ground. Her belly dropped the way it did when she drove too fast over a hill.

"Good. Take it nice and slow," he said.

Skylar did it again. She hovered in place for a moment, understanding what he meant by balance. The two wings had to move in sync and her legs had to be still, or she tilted one way or the other.

"Keep your head in place."

Cautiously, Skylar pulled her huge body a few more feet off the ground, focusing on her balance.

"Good. I'll show you a few things." He trotted away to put distance between them. "Trust your wings. They feel flimsy until you're in the air."

Skylar dropped to the ground, watching in interest as he slid the sweats down past the tight globes of his ass, thick thighs and lean calves. She grimaced and looked away when he changed shape, now knowing just how painful it was.

When he was done, he unfurled his wings and shook them out then approached her, nuzzling her with his long snout.

She rubbed her cheek along his and down his neck, fascinated by the sensitivity of her skin and the feel of his smooth scales gliding beneath hers. Chace nudged her in return then took a step back, lifting himself into the air above the meadow with ease.

Skylar studied him, watching how he held himself and balanced. She tried to do the same and climbed tentatively into the air, not at all certain she wanted to be so far from the ground. She was wobbly at best, her balance little better than it had been when she tried rollerblading once before. She focused hard on keeping her wings moving as a unit.

Chace lifted himself higher and began circling. Skylar did so as well, her heart flipping in her chest when the first wind current knocked her off balance. She teetered, eyes on the ground a few meters below, and then caught herself.

Flying clenched in Chace's or Gavin's claws was frightening enough. Knowing she was the only thing standing between her and falling? Terrifying. She didn't feel in control enough of her new body to perform any of the aerial feats she'd seen Chace do.

For hours, she followed his lead, learning to balance her body weight and use her wings to maneuver through the sky. In early afternoon, she caught a whiff of something that made her snort.

Chace was already looking in the direction from which the smell came, and he hovered in midair, assessing.

Skylar wasn't able to identify what it was. An animal of some sort, she guessed, but she couldn't pinpoint what based solely on smell. It was difficult for her to tap into her Protector senses when her focus was on staying in flight. She wasn't able to figure out if it was a shifter, let alone identify the signature of which shifter it was.

Chace tossed his head towards the cabin and wheeled, soaring back in that direction. Skylar followed him, nose wrinkling at the scent. He circled the meadow and landed gently. She followed suit.

Sensing he wanted to talk, she concentrated on shifting quickly. It seemed slower when going from animal to human, and she closed her eyes, waiting for the pain.

Hot agony spun through her. She didn't fight it but descended into a haze of pain. It left her exhausted and relieved a few minutes later.

"You really gotta shift faster," Chace advised. He knelt beside her, clothed once again in his sweatpants. "It hurts less that way."

"I'm working on it." She sighed and sat.

He handed her a t-shirt, and she tugged it on, eyes falling to his muscular chest. Instinctively she reached out to touch him, loving the way his skin felt beneath her fingers. His scent was intoxicating, a sweet, smoky perfume that wrapped around her senses and made her want to climb into his arms.

"What was that?" she asked, glancing upward.

Chace took her hand and held it. "Griffin."

"They smell awful!"

"Definitely." He snorted. "They've been hovering around for a while. They can sense us outside the cabin. We need to leave before they work up the nerve to attack us."

"Um, no," she said, eyeing him. "We're supposed to do the opposite. I need to stop Dillon."

Chace's eyebrows went up. "How?"

"I want to talk to him first."

"So you'll just *ask* him to stop whatever it is he's doing?" His gaze was intense, his doubt clear.

"I've got to start somewhere," she said. *And I will find out what happened to my mother.* "Besides, things are different now that you have your magic back and I have a better idea what I can do."

"Skylar." Chace's frown was deep.

"This is what I'm supposed to do," she replied firmly.

"Put yourself back in the line of fire? You barely survived him the first two times, and it's going to take time for you to learn to use the skills each shifter has."

"I'm the Protector, aren't I?" she said with an upbeat smile. "Besides, you'll be there with me." Without waiting for any more objections, she rose and walked back to the cabin.

Chace followed, his unhappiness palpable. Skylar pulled off her shirt to put on a bra. His muscular arms wrapped around her, and he pulled her into his solid, warm body. He'd taken off the sweats, and she felt his thick, hard arousal pressed against her backside.

"I can't let anything happen to you again," he whispered into her hair.

She sighed and rested her head against his shoulder for a moment, tracing her fingers along the roped muscles of his forearm.

"It would kill me, Sky."

"I know, Chace. We'll work together this time. There's nothing that can take down two of us," she said. "But I know we have to do this. We have to protect those who deserve it and put those to sleep who threaten that peace."

"You are the sweetest and bravest person I know." He squeezed her closer. "I'll go to the ends of the earth with you."

You just may have to.

"Or to the shower," he added with a hungry growl.

Skylar's body was already humming with need for her mate. Twisting in his arms, she gazed up at him, astounded she had *this* to look forward to every morning she awoke for the rest of her life. His noble, chiseled features were softened by the tenderness of his blue gaze, and she tucked a lock of his blond hair behind his ear. Lust and dragon fire were in his eyes, but something else was, too, an emotion so deep and warm, it made her tear up.

"You do love me, don't you?" she whispered. "I can see it."

"Maybe a little."

She laughed in delight.

Chace captured her mouth with his, his hot kiss deep and demanding.

Skylar melted against him, loving the way his muscular frame felt beneath her fingers. Skimming his body with her hands, she reached between them to stroke his dick hard.

He groaned. "Shower?"

"Yeah," she said breathlessly.

With a wolfish grin, Chace grabbed her hand and pulled her into the bathroom. The shower was small for two people, but she knew the point wasn't to get clean anyway. The cabin had turned it on for them in advance, and the mirror was already fogged up.

Closing the glass door behind them, Chace pressed her back against the wall, moving his hips against hers. The shock of cold tile and warm water made her gasp and shiver, the sensations in her body more intense than ever before.

His kiss was hard, his hands traveling down her body to her ass. He lifted her, and she wrapped her legs around his hips. Pressed between him and the tile wall, she circled his neck with her hands and waited for the pleasure she knew was coming.

Chace entered her slowly, inch by inch, pushing her against the wall while kissing her deeply. His hot tongue explored her mouth then traveled over her lips before he began pressing kisses down her jaw.

"Oh, god yes!" she groaned when he was all the way in. "You feel incredible!"

"So do you," he replied huskily. "Always so wet." He moved inside her a few times, and she gripped him hard with her arms and thighs. One of his hands slid between them to stroke her clit.

Skylar shuddered at the exquisite pleasure the light touch caused. She moved against him, needing him too much to think of anything else. Nibbling on his ear, she clung to him.

"I love you, Chace," she whispered.

His movement stilled, and he pulled back far enough to see her face. He smoothed her hair away from her features, his intense gaze burning.

"Do you really?" he asked. "Even after everything?"

With him inside her and their bodies pressed together, she'd never felt surer of anything.

"I do." She traced the planes of his face with her fingertips.

Water poured over them. Chace eased out of her then stepped back.

Uncertain how to read his actions and sudden quietness, she lowered her legs and gazed up at him, her arms around his neck.

"Will you say it again?" he asked hoarsely.

Skylar smiled, understanding fluttering through her. Her dragon, the most incredible man in the world, had never known the love of another or what it was like to share something like a heart or soul. He'd been alone his entire life. Until now.

"I love you, Chace." She said it more loudly and looked him straight in the eye. "You're my dragon."

He rested his forehead against hers, his eyes closing. They stood in the shower in intimate quiet, the tension between them thick, but the emotion even thicker.

"You're my Sky." His voice was uneven and thick. "I love you, too, Skylar."

Sensing how vulnerable he was in that moment, she slid her palms up to take his face then kissed him hard. Desire quickly turned into something more intense and primal. Their tongues tangled desperately, their hands roaming each other's bodies with urgency.

Chace spun her and pressed her against the wall with his upper body weight, entering the depths of her body quickly. The jarring cold of the tile startled her into greater awareness of the sensations filling her body. One of his hands traveled down her wet body to her clit and began stroking her lightly, fast.

"Say it again," he ordered in her ear, thrusting into her with the desperation she, too, felt.

"I love you!" she cried.

Her orgasm rose hot and fast, egged on by the friction of his dick against her G-spot and the tickle of his fingers around her clit. He filled her in a way unlike any she'd ever experienced, completed her world as if he'd always been there.

"I love you, too, Sky," he said, his breathing ragged.

She moaned, his honey-bonfire scent and the wicked movement of his fingers driving her beyond herself.

Seconds later, she shattered. Waves of intense pleasure flew through her, wringing a throaty shout from her.

Chace withdrew and spun her once more, hefting her onto his hips again. He kissed her hungrily and plunged into the seizing depths of her core hard and fast while pressing her back against the wall.

Skylar groaned once more, her orgasm extended by the friction of his hard dick inside her sensitive sheathe. She clung to him, clawing at his back and forcing his body closer with her legs.

"I ... love you, too ... Sky ..." he said a split second before he, too, gave a cry of release. He slowed but continued to pump then buried his dick deep inside her and stayed.

Panting, the two of them were still as warm water cascaded down from the rain showerhead in the ceiling. Chace's body quivered from his release, his fingers gripping and releasing her ass as he worked through his pleasure.

Skylar didn't have to hide her tears of joy in the shower. She let them fall and hugged him to her hard, breathing in the scent of a dragon while clinging to the frame of a man.

"We're doing this every morning," he said at last without lifting his head.

She laughed, unable to identify a time where she'd felt so comfortable.

Like I've found my home.

"And maybe every evening, too," he added.

"I think we need a vacation when this is over. You still owe me a pizza date," she reminded him.

He raised his head and gazed down at her, the glow in his eyes making more tears spill. She smiled.

"Was I too rough?" he asked, concerned. He released her and

withdrew, stepping back until he had enough room to wrap his arms around her.

"No," she murmured. Skylar hugged him hard. His soft skin was warm, the hard muscles beneath it strong and solid. She rested her ear against his heart and listened to it beat, knowing she was the reason it did so.

"You're shaking."

"I've never been this happy before, Chace," she told him and buried her face into his shoulder.

He held her more tightly.

"I love you. I don't want to lose you. Ever," she whispered. "It makes me fear what's coming even more."

He lifted her chin and gazed down at her. With the tenderness was a new emotion: resolution.

"You have nothing to fear. We have each other, and we know what we're supposed to do: put the shifter community back together and take care of everyone," he said firmly. "I love you with every ounce of my soul. I'll always be there for you, no matter what happens. You can trust me, Skylar."

"I do." She smiled, touched by his words.

"We have a world to conquer." His thumb drifted across her plump lips, and his gaze dropped to her mouth. "Then we'll come right back here and fuck until we can't walk anymore."

Skylar laughed again. They stood in comfortable silence for a moment, enjoying each other's presence.

"Come on," he said reluctantly. "Let's get the show started, so we can spend more time together." He opened the door to the shower.

Skylar grudgingly went. She dried off then left the bathroom, headed to a pile of her clothes. As if to remind her of how serious their awaiting adventure was, the lasso sat in the center of her clothing.

Her thoughts sobered quickly at the sight of it and the thought of what they had to do. She glanced towards the bathroom and found Chace in the doorway, studying her.

"You okay?" he asked gently.

"Yeah." She smiled quickly and started to dress. "I want to help everyone, Chace. I know my father didn't believe that, but I think we can."

"I think you'll find there are some people beyond reason." He moved towards his dresser as he spoke.

"Like Dillon?"

"I imagine there are others as well. Your father wasn't budging from his view of the world. Some people are too entrenched."

"Or too motivated to get their ways," she murmured, thoughts going to another dragon. Skylar pulled on her shirt. "Like Freyja."

Chace froze for a moment then resumed dressing.

Interesting. "She's behind all this. Brainwashing me, causing the war between shifters."

"I guess I'm not surprised." His tone was measured. "Gavin was right about someone trying to push the strong shifters out of the way?"

"Yes. Mason won't tell me everything, but he did say she hasn't give up on her plan, even though the initial one didn't work." Skylar pushed her feet into her boots then bent over to tie them.

When she straightened, Chace's features were hard to read. He seemed pensive, troubled almost.

"Is that an issue?" she asked, disappointed to know there was some emotion remaining after so long.

"Not for me," he replied. "Might be for *us*, though. She's not the kind of person who is going to change her mind. And she was able to reach out to others enough to strategize when she was supposed to be in hibernation. It means we may not have much of an option, if she refuses to back down."

"You think we'll have to kill her." Skylar's voice was hushed.

"I think it's possible."

Not quite what I was expecting. "Dillon, too, maybe." She grew still. "I've always known I might have to kill someone. I thought it'd be a shifter, back when I thought they were my enemies. Do you think we have any sort of obligation to try to work things out in a way that spares people's lives, even if they really deserve to be taken out?"

Chace glanced at her.

"I mean, because we're leading the community now," she added.

"I think we need to do whatever it takes to ensure the safety of the community. No matter what that entails," he said quietly. "This is new territory for me, too, Sky, but I think we must always do what is best for the shifters as a whole."

She nodded. Never in all her time did she think she'd be in this position, the unofficial shifter queen, charged with making hard calls to protect the very people she once hunted. She felt neither worthy nor prepared, but she was grateful to have Chace with her throughout it all.

"And … as for us. Are we good?" she asked uncertainly.

"Absolutely," he replied without hesitation. "We're in this together."

She believed him. They were too different to see eye-to-eye on everything, but she hoped they were able to build on their relationship to work through those differences while guiding the shifters into a more peaceful era.

"Do Protectors live as long as shifters?" she asked curiously.

"I'm not sure. I don't see why you couldn't, since you pretty much *are* a shifter."

She stuck her tongue out at him, not liking the reminder.

"Even if you don't for some reason …" he continued, hushed. "Sky, I've lost everyone I ever cared about. At one point, it made me harden myself to the world."

She studied him as he spoke, hearing the pain in his voice.

"But with you … I can't live without you. I don't *want* to live without you. I'd rather spend eighty years together and eternity with the knowledge that my best years were with my Sky than walk away and never know how incredible it is to be with you," he said softly. "I guess we'll find out. Either way, I'll never, ever regret you, Sky, or take advantage of every second we spend together."

Her eyes misted at the sweet words, and she ducked her head, the giddiness inside her wanting to explode with happiness.

"Now, let's see what we got waiting for us!" he said with forced lightness and opened the door to the cabin.

Turning her mind to their mission, she followed him outside. She smelled fire the moment she stepped onto the porch and sought out the source. Black smoke rolled into the sky from the direction of Mason's hideout.

"Chace …" she murmured.

"I see it. Want a ride?"

She nodded, trusting his wings more than hers.

He stripped and shifted, turning into the magnificent teal dragon that once terrified her. With a tight smile, she rubbed the soft spot between his nostrils then stood back when he took flight.

Chace picked her up gently and soared into the sky, staying a few feet above the treetops as he made his way towards the base where Mason had taken her. She saw the damage before they reached it: the compound was on fire, along with the forest around it. Her senses picked up on the shifters in the vicinity, and she cataloged them quickly. Four alive, over a dozen dead.

Mason was among the living.

Chace found a nearby meadow and lowered them into it. The moment her feet hit the ground, she was running towards the shifters she sensed were alive, assured that Chace would be at her heels as soon as he shifted. Her heart pounded and her hands trembled from concern that was too strong to be anything other than one of her newfound instincts. She didn't even know these shifters, and she was terrified for them.

"Mason!" she cried, reaching a picnic area near the lake.

Smoke ballooned overhead. The breeze was carrying it in the direction opposite her, but it filled the sky.

Forcing herself to focus on her shifter senses, she picked up on the lion shifter and altered her course. He and the others were close to the lake.

Skylar pushed through trees to reach the opening around a cluster of boulders and tree stumps. The four living shifters she sensed were present covered in soot and ash.

She slowed when she reached them, assessing them quickly. None of them appeared to be too badly wounded.

"Mason, what happened?" she demanded, sinking onto the ground beside him.

The lion shifter appeared exhausted. His clothing was torn and charred in spots, and there was blood on his arms and chest.

"Something I didn't expect," he admitted with a sigh. "Dillon and Freyja teamed up. I think things are about to get nasty."

"Teamed up?" she echoed, astonished. "They hate each other!"

"But they hate you more," he said, meeting her gaze. "Think about it. With the legit leaders of the shifters coming into power, what could be worse? I just wish ..." His gaze clouded and a look of agony crossed his features. "These were the only ones I could save." His whisper was so low, she barely heard it.

Skylar's gaze skimmed over the other three. They, too, showed the signs of having gone though a war zone. Her thoughts grew darker as she considered the dozen that didn't make it.

What if she and Chace had tried to stop Dillon instead of spending the night together? Was this her fault? Was she already failing in her role as the Protector?

Guilt trickled through her. She's been so happy to have her dragon back, she hadn't thought twice about what Dillon and Freyja might do or the risk they posed to the rest of the people she was supposed to be protecting.

"They're completely insane," she said. "Do they think this will inspire other shifters to follow them?"

"They probably think it'll prevent shifters from following *you*," Mason replied.

Because I couldn't save their lives. Her jaw clenched. Skylar sank into her thoughts for a moment, unable to fathom the idea of people dying around her, because she wasn't able to help them. It was the reason she'd worked so hard as a slayer – to protect innocent humans from dangerous dragons – only to discover the truth about who she was. Her instinct to protect others had always been present.

"I need to find them," she said and rose.

"And do what?" Mason asked.

"Stop them. Somehow. I've still got one lasso. I can put them to sleep."

"I think it's too late for that, Sky."

She glanced at him, not liking the ominous note in his voice.

"They're splitting the community between those who are afraid to oppose them and those who are hoping you and Chace can help. Once they've eliminated the opposition, the war between Dillon and Freyja will start again. No one will be left standing."

She'd come to a similar conclusion. Chace was right: Freyja and Dillon had to be stopped, at any cost. She had to be ready for everything that entailed, even if it meant doing something she'd hoped not to in order to stop them from hurting people.

"I can find any shifter from a mountain," she said. "I promise you, Mason, we'll figure out how to stop them."

"Chace can take you up."

"Yes. He's ..." *right behind me.* She turned all the way around. She neither heard nor saw him.

In fact, her Protector senses and the fire in her blood told her he wasn't anywhere near her.

"What the hell is going on?" she muttered, exploring the instincts with impatience. "He was here and now he's ..." *With Freyja.*

A new emotion rose within her, hot and quick. Why was her lover with his ex?

Skylar shook her head, not about to go down that path, despite the suspicious circumstances. No, she had more important issues right now. If he was with Freyja, she had to assume something was wrong.

She texted Chace quickly, knowing he'd respond if he was able to.

"You." She turned to the Pegasus shifter resting against a stump.

"Can you fly?"

He nodded.

"Don't do anything without a plan, Sky," Mason warned.

She hesitated, grappling with her emotions. She was torn between wanting to find Chace and pursuing Dillon before anyone else got hurt. Chace was no longer vulnerable. If he left her side, it was for a good reason, and he was the most capable person she knew when it came to taking care of himself. Why not tell her though? After yesterday, did he still feel the need to prove himself by taking care of the Freyja issue? Or had Freyja tricked him somehow?

Trust him.

She paced. Concern messed with her ability to think logically, and she took a deep breath, pushing it aside.

"Even if ... something is wrong, and Chace is in trouble ..." The words made her gut twist into knots. Shaking her head, she continued. "They still want me. That's been the constant. It seems like the best way to draw them out is to open a dialogue."

"Yeah. But you want to get them on your territory."

"I don't have territory!" she exclaimed.

"The desert near The Field, where the shifters are. The bar is still there, and so are about two hundred shifters that are loyal to you and Chace. You freed over half of them from hibernation, and Chace provided refuge at the bar for the rest," Mason pointed out. "If you want to dangle a piece of meat in front of them, do it where you've got numbers."

She rubbed her face. *Focus, Sky!* Mason was right. No matter what was happening to Chace right now, she had to find a way to knock Dillon and Freyja off balance, to pull them into the open and capture them. Any danger Chace was in would be neutralized without the two strongest shifters able to contain him. She'd lasso the two troublemakers.

Or kill them. Chace's insistence it might be the only way to prevent more deaths made her feel a little ill.

"We need the dragons," she murmured and glanced at her watch.

It was almost noon. They had a long wait before the nocturnal shifters would be out. "Come on. We need to warn the others, if nothing else."

Mason nodded. The Pegasus shifter rose wearily and moved a few feet away to shift.

Skylar watched, mind racing. Chace had his magic back. He was more than able to fight off or escape from either Dillon or Freyja.

Why, then, had he voluntarily gone with one of them?

She didn't like the ache in her breast, the one that made her recall that the man she was in love with had once betrayed her.

You can trust me, Skylar. The tender look on his face when he said the words made any doubt she had about him melt. She didn't know what was compelling enough for him to walk away from her without so much as a farewell, but whatever the reason, she was going to trust him. *He did dive off a cliff to save me,* she reminded herself. And told her he loved her then proved it in how he made love to her.

She pulled out her phone and texted him. *Everything all right?*

"I can carry one of you," the Pegasus shifter said.

"I can carry another, I think," Skylar added.

"No offense, Sky, but I'm not riding with you," Mason said. "Not until I can see with my own eyes you know how to fly."

"I'm learning."

"Oh, hell no. We'll drive. That way we all reach the place alive, even if Dillon kills us soon after."

Skylar sighed, frustrated with her Protector skill. One day, it'd be an incredible one to have. But for now, she was stuck between knowing what it was and not being able to wield it well enough to help them.

Chapter Nine

MILES AWAY, CHACE LANDED beside the great silver-white dragon at the base of a mountain about an hour flight from the meadow where he'd left Sky. The door in the stone before him was camouflaged by boulders that rendered it impossible to spot from the sky. There were no roads nearby or any trace that anyone had ever been here. It was a perfect place to keep something hidden from a dragon.

He shifted and dressed, watching as Freyja did the same.

She was as beautiful as she had been in the dream and as he recalled from their short time together so long ago. Her smile was cold and didn't reach her eyes. She dressed in leggings and a tunic, her blonde hair reaching the small of her back.

When she'd appeared out of the forest an hour ago, after taking Skylar to a field near the compound. He'd been ready to tear Freyja limb from limb on sight. He was certain there was nothing she could say to keep him from doing it, either. And then she spoke. One simple sentence turned his world around.

I know where Sky's mother is.

How could he *not* follow her here?

Chace watched Freyja approach the stone door and type in a code on a keypad. He glanced down at his phone and saw that Skylar had texted.

I'm good. Be there soon. Don't start without me, he replied then tucked the phone away.

"You were really busy for someone who was supposed to be hibernating," he stated.

"I failed with you. I wasn't going to fail with her," she replied. "It took some work and help from others like Dillon, but I succeeded."

"I never doubted your determination." *Your heart is another matter.* "So you attack Mason to lure us out then bring me here."

"I don't need Mason or his kind anymore," she said. "I do need you, Chace."

"And Sky."

"Either one of you can get rid of my Dillon issue."

The bolts to the door clicked, and she pulled the heavy door open. Freyja disappeared into the darkness beyond.

Chace trailed warily. He suspected he was being set up. But with his magic back, he had nothing to fear. Once he saw whatever it was Freyja wanted to show him, he'd return to Sky.

Hopefully with news about her mother. He'd witness the expression on her face whenever she mentioned her family, a sense of loss he understood after almost losing her. If there were any way to save Skylar the pain that came from not knowing, he'd find a way to do it, even if that meant following Freyja into a potential trap.

The dark tunnel leading beneath the mountain was narrow and short, the ceiling an inch or two above his head. He saw a faint glow indicating a perpendicular hallway and the ghost-like figure of Freyja walking ahead of him.

She turned towards the light, and he followed. A heavy door was on either side of the shallow hallway, and the light came from the crack beneath one.

Freyja typed in a code on a keypad on the wall beside the door opposite the lighted room then entered, triggering a motion sensitive light.

Chace walked into the steel vault. It was tiny, about three meters by three meters, with a pedestal in the center upon which a floodlight shone. A single shifter figurine was in the center of the pedestal. His heart slowed, and he was almost afraid to hope that the human statue half the size of his thumb was the mother Skylar had been searching for her whole life. He felt both honored and concerned at the idea of doing something so incredible for the other half of his heart.

"Is that her?" he asked in a hushed voice.

"As far as you know."

His anger stirred, and he faced Freyja.

"I don't do anything for free, Chace," she said. Her arms were crossed, her pale gaze on him.

"What do you want?" he snapped.

"Dillon's head."

He rolled his eyes. "You're a *dragon.* Go get it yourself!"

"Slight problem with that. Right now, we're allies working together to ensure the shifters don't flock to you and your Protector. I can't openly oppose him."

"You want me to eliminate the competition." He considered. On the surface, Dillon's death suited his purpose as well. With the leader of the griffins out of the way, Sky was one step closer to stopping the war between dragons and griffins. "What's stopping me from leaving here with her mother and killing you both?"

"The challenge of being a Protector away from her guardian." Freyja smiled. "She's vulnerable. The griffins are tracking her, and you left her alone. They have orders to kill the Protector in an hour, if I don't tell them otherwise. Agree to my terms, and I'll have them stand down."

"It's not in your interest to spare her." He carefully avoided showing Freyja she'd found a pressure point. Any suggestion that Sky was in danger made him want to rip off the head of anyone standing between him and her, sweep Sky up and take her to the safety of his lair. While he doubted the griffins could get her, he hated the idea he'd contributed to her danger by leaving her.

Half of Sky's danger is standing before me, he reminded himself.

"I didn't go through all this trouble to kill her now. I can still use her magic to rule the shifters. But if Dillon kills off the shifters before I can stop him, I'll have nothing left to rule over," Freyja continued.

Chace studied the figurine, half-listening. It was similar to the ones he and Skylar had found at Caleb's house and awoken from hibernation, with the exception he'd never seen a human among all the hundreds of stone statues. He really had no way of knowing if it was Skylar's mother or not without waking the sleeping statue. If it was, and he had a chance to save her, what did he tell Skylar if he walked away?

If it wasn't, and this was an elaborate plan to trap him and Skylar both …

"Bring me his head, and you can take Sky's mother with you."

On the surface, it sounded like a good idea. He had every intention of taking out Dillon anyway. All he had to do was leave here, find the griffin, kill him and return. It would solve one of Skylar's problems as well.

Freyja never does anything that doesn't benefit her. He sought some explanation or theory as to why he had the feeling this deal was too good to be true. Without their leader, the griffins would be easier to capture and place into hibernation. He'd have to deal with Freyja either way eventually.

And he'd be able to deliver an answer to Skylar about what happened to her mother.

"Bring you his head," he repeated slowly. "You call off the griffins and I leave her with her mother."

"I want what's best for the shifters, Chace," she said. "All I've done has been to make our community stronger. I never hurt the shifters that got killed. That was all Dillon and Caleb."

"I really don't care. You tried to brainwash Sky and the others and made them hunt down their own kind," he growled. "The damage you've done is irreparable and you're still determined to get rid of the rightful leaders of the community. Is there any chance you'll fall in line and be grateful we spared you when this is over? Or will I have to come for your head next?"

Anger flashed across her features. "Neither of those things will happen!" she snapped. "Neither you nor that *girl* are fit to lead the shifters. The dragons will fall in line behind me, and I will order them to destroy as many shifters and humans as it takes to force you to back off!"

That's the Freyja I know. The same dragon that was either lying about the figurine being Skylar's mother or who would crush it while he was gone.

"You know what? Do your own dirty work," he said.

"So you'll just let Skylar die?"

Even knowing she was messing with him, he couldn't stop the flare of dragon fire that raced through him. "You underestimate her. She's the most incredible woman I've ever met, and she's got a ton of shifters willing to ally with her." *I'll be back with her in all of two seconds anyway.* He turned his back before Freyja could see he really was worried. Chace strode to the pedestal and snatched the figurine. "I'll be leaving with her mother – or whoever this is – as well."

Too late, his instincts warned him. He heard the heavy metal door behind him swing shut, trapping him in the vault.

Chace spun and eyed the door. He crossed to it and planted his hands on the cool steel. The walls were stone and were a good two feet thick. He determined quickly that shifting without careful deliberation about his size might pose more of a danger than waiting. If he shifted too large, he'd either end up crushed by the tiny space or might get luck and knock the walls out.

Furious at himself for not being more cautious, he dropped back next to the pedestal then opened his closed fist.

"Who are you?" he whispered at the figurine. In theory, Skylar should be the one to awaken her mother.

Unless it was a trick, in which case, it would get her hopes up for no reason.

After a moment of thought, he clenched his hand around the figurine and counted to ten.

The figure changed from stone black to flesh colored. He set it on the ground and moved away, excitement and dread darting through him. Chace watched carefully, unable to shake his growing hope that being trapped here was going to be worth it.

The human grew quickly, and he was soon able to discern the shapely hips belonging to a woman.

A naked woman.

"Oh, shit." Chace turned away awkwardly, uncertain how he was supposed to act around the mother of his love. Leering at her was out of the question, but he needed to make sure he had the right person, too. He waited, wary of any sort of attack, and listened to the sounds of her body changing shapes.

She groaned in either pain or relief. He wasn't certain. The sounds of her shifting stopped. On edge with an unknown person behind him, his dragon senses followed her movements. It didn't take looking at her to determine she wasn't a threat. He heard her sit and sigh and the chatter of her teeth. She was cold or maybe in shock. His senses were tingling, but he wasn't yet certain what it meant.

He cleared his throat. "Can I ask who you are?" he ventured.

Her movement stilled and her breath caught, as if she didn't realize someone else was present.

"Dragon?" she whispered in a hoarse voice. "You're a dragon."

"Yeah," he said. "You?"

"No. I mean ..." She sounded confused. "My name is Ginger. Who are you?"

"Chace."

"Where am I, dragon?"

Ginger. The name of Skylar's mother. Chace struggled to remain still, wanting more than anything to sweep up the scared woman into a hug then fly off and drop her in Skylar's lap.

"We're somewhat trapped under a mountain," he said with some amusement. "Can I give you my shirt?"

She muttered a curse under her breath, as if she didn't realize she was naked either.

He smiled faintly and peeled off his sweatshirt, holding it out behind him.

She snatched it. A few seconds later, she spoke. "Okay. I'm good enough."

Chace turned, not certain what to expect.

Ginger was shaved bald and pale. She was about Skylar's size with dazzling blue eyes and the same shape of face. She appeared to be exhausted and trembled on her feet, his sweatshirt falling to mid-thigh.

For a moment, he wasn't able to speak. Based on appearances alone, she was too similar not to be related to Skylar. His gaze went to her baldhead.

She flushed, anger sparking in her eyes. She reached for her head. "They used it to make another lasso."

"Really?"

"The blood and hair of a Protector. It's all that will work on shifters. But it means they hunt you down and try to kill you." She hugged herself and leaned against the wall. "They drained me near death before putting me into hibernation."

"They kept you alive," he voiced softly, head cocked to the side.

"To bring me back and do it again. It takes a lot of blood to do what they were planning. They woke me up a few times during my hibernation." Her gaze grew distant. She appeared to be thinking. Her shoulders sagged. "I can't feel him. He's gone, isn't he?"

"Gavin?"

She nodded.

"Yes." Chace cleared his throat, not certain how to deal with a woman who was realizing she had lost the other half of her heart. It would crush him. *It did crush me!* He sought out something to ease her pain. "Skylar is alive."

Ginger appeared shocked. Her mouth dropped open, and for a moment, she wasn't able to speak.

"If I can get us out of here, I'll take you to her," he offered. He went to the door again, assessing the frame.

"My Sky is alive?" Ginger managed at last. "You're sure? You've seen her?"

"Yeah. She's fine. All fire and no sense."

Ginger gave a gleeful laugh. "Gavin used to say the same about me! Are you her dragon?"

"I am," he said more quietly. "Right now, we need to get out of here before Freyja comes back."

"Sky's alive."

He glanced over his shoulder at the tender note in Ginger's voice. Her eyes sparkled with tears, her smile large. He understood that feeling, the swelling of one's heart and the sensation of being close to exploding with emotion for someone else. His own throat tightened as he thought of how recently he'd felt such an overwhelming emotion.

He faced the door again. "Just ... don't cry. I'm not really good at handling that," he said uncomfortably.

"Okay." Her whisper was so much like Sky's, when she was trying to be brave. It made a part of him melt.

"Trust me. We'll get out of here." Chace stood back for a moment, pensive. *I'm not about to fail Skylar now after all we've been through.*

Ginger sat down and was still.

Chace paced in the small space of the tiny room, already knowing what he'd have to do to get out. He wished he'd considered that before waking up Ginger, in case he wasn't able to control his magic, and ended up crushing both of them. If Skylar was there, she might be able to pick up the magic of other nearby shifters, beasts that might be better prepared to smashing through a metal door.

Skylar.

"Can I ask you something?" He spun, regarding Ginger closely. "Can you shift?"

She shook her head. "From what I was able to learn about Protectors in the short time I was one, each one has a different gift meant to help the community."

"What's yours?"

"Nothing useful." She sighed. "I can cloak shifters. Except it didn't work on Gavin all the time. We think he was too strong or too old. Every once in a while, someone was able to pick him up, and they were aggressive. I hid Sky and me for thirteen years with varying success."

"That's an amazing ability," Chace said, thoughts going to how easy it was for their enemies to track them, now that Sky's Protector magic was working. She was like a brilliant, glowing beacon to every shifter on the planet, and so was he. "How does it work?"

She lifted her head from her arms. He pitied her for a moment. She was weak to the point of frail, and he suspected she'd need to be taken somewhere safe the moment he escaped rather than into the middle of a battle with griffins.

Cabin can take care of her. I just have to get us out.

"Easy." She showed him her palm. "I touch you and will your magic to be quiet. It shields you, and no one can find you."

"You've given me a crazy idea," he said with a rueful smile. "Sky can shift into any creature that's near her and ends up big enough to kick their ass."

"That's so wonderful." Ginger smiled. "She was a spirited, determined little girl. She wanted her own dragon so she could fly." Her gaze lingered on her. "You seem like a good man, Chace."

He said nothing, aware the opposite was true. Not wanting to dwell on his past failings, he looked away and studied the door.

"Can you quiet the magic in other ways?" he asked. "Like, if I shift into a dragon to take out this door, can you keep me from crushing us both?"

"It worked with Gavin." Her smile grew sad.

Chace wasn't certain what to say in the heavy silence that followed. Was it his place to tell her what happened? Or should he leave it to Sky?

This whole sensitivity to others thing is way too complicated. He almost knew Skylar and Gunner well enough to know when he should say something. But strangers? Especially *this* stranger? Trying to figure it out made him want to fly as fast and far as he could to escape the pressure of someone else's expectations.

Instead of addressing what happened, he decided to get them the hell away from Freyja before she came back with Dillon to eliminate him.

"Alrighty. I'm gonna shift. This is awkward, but I'm not sure what to think of being naked in front of my mate's mother," he said. It was the first time in his life he'd ever thought to be self-conscious.

She laughed, gaze sparkling. "You're my Sky's dragon, which makes you a son to me. I don't care, Chace. I've seen my fair share of naked shifters."

He nodded curtly and pulled off his t-shirt, ordering his body to begin shifting before he stripped out of his pants. A glance at Ginger revealed she was looking away politely – but with amusement. He saw the same spirit that Skylar had in the half-smile and couldn't help marveling at what he'd done.

He'd found the answer Skylar risked her life more than once to discover. He'd never been as humbled or proud as he was in that moment.

Or scared that Ginger might not make it out of there alive.

His body began to grow out of control almost at once, too large and fast for the size of the room. Just as quickly, Ginger placed a hand on his shoulder, and his magic did as she said it would: calmed to a point where he was able to dictate his size. Despite her help, he smashed the pedestal in the center with his body.

When he was transformed, there was barely space for Ginger in the room. His head and shoulders were hunched down near the ground and his tail tucked between his legs, its tip flicking back and forth beneath his nose.

Maybe a little too big, he judged. With a nudge at Ginger, he waited for her to move to a corner before turning to face the door.

Chace slammed his shoulder into the metal door. It shuddered in the doorframe but held. He did it again and pushed with all his might. Dust puffed out from the edges as he managed to shove the door two inches.

But it didn't give the way he expected it to.

He moved back until his rump hit the back wall. Motioning for Ginger to get behind him, he lifted his head and summoned his fire. It bloomed in his chest and traveled up his throat, filling his nostrils with the familiar scent of a bonfire.

Unleashing it at the door, he blew until he was breathless and the door glowed red. The room had grown hot quickly.

"You better ... hurry," Ginger said. She coughed in the thick smoke, and he sensed she wasn't going to last long in the furnace-like conditions of the vault.

Chace smashed his shoulder into the door once more, grimacing at the pain. The outer layer of metal was soft and gave easily, but the core of the steel door was still solid. He braced his back legs against the rear wall and shoved through the molten metal. The door began to give, inch by inch. With another deep breath, he shoved harder.

The door snapped out of its place and sailed across the hallway. Smoke poured out into the dark hall, and Chace sat back, panting with effort. His shoulders were too wide for him to leave the vault. Ginger was coughing and started past him into the hallway, but he blocked her path with a leg.

There was no way to know who or what was waiting for them in the hallway. Ordering himself to shift, he took her arm and pulled her down to the floor, where a thin layer of air existed beneath the smoke.

"It'll clear out soon," he whispered. "Stay here until I clear a path. Okay?"

Coughing, she nodded.

Chace snagged his t-shirt then hauled on his jeans before darting into the smoke-filled hallway. He heard movements, and somewhere, an alarm sounded. It was followed by the distant sound of what sounded like muffled explosions.

Explosions under a mountain ... Chace's stomach filled with dread. Freyja was taking no chances that he escaped.

The door across from the vault was open, rendering the smoke yellow in the warm light. He sensed only one person in the room – a human by the scent.

He stretched his dragon senses and ducked a split second before someone's foot arced through the air where his head had been. Chace grabbed the man around the waist and shoved him into the stone wall, punching him twice. His attacker dropped silently.

The roaring squawk of a griffin filled the hallway, and he froze for a split second. He was able to reach both sides of the hallway by stretching out his arms, and it was too low for him to stand up straight without the ceiling tickling his hair.

No room to shift.

The ground rumbled beneath him, confirming his suspicion that Freyja had built in a secondary means of ensuring he didn't leave if the vault failed.

"Shit!" He paused in front of the doorway, unfazed by the smoke. "Ginger, come on!"

She scrambled after him, choking on the smoke and waving it away. He took her arm and placed her solidly behind him.

"I can't shift in here, and there's something pretty big between us and the exit, not to mention I'm pretty sure the mountain is about to come down on top of us."

Her breathing was erratic, the hands touching his back shaking. She steadied her body against him. The ground was shaking, and dust added to the smoke in the air.

Was she strong enough to make it out of there before the whole mountain collapsed on top of them?

"Stay with me, okay?" he said. "If anything happens, run and use your magic power to hide yourself."

"I won't leave you," she replied firmly.

"Like hell you won't. If I say run, you run."

She said nothing, and he sensed she'd already made up her mind, as stubborn as her daughter. Chace gritted his teeth. A small griffin was able to fit in the hallway ahead of them, but a dragon was going to get stuck if he tried.

Which meant he'd have to be smart or risk being shredded. Skylar had lost one parent; he wasn't going to let anything happen to her mother.

"Let's do this," he whispered. "As quietly as possible."

He started forward, keeping to one side of the shallow hallway and using his dragon senses to guide them. The griffin squawked again, this time closer, at the mouth of the hallway. Though dark, the form of the beast in the white-grey smoke was like a dark blob. Chace eased towards the intersection, not about to spend more time than necessary trapped in the hallway and risk running into a few more griffins before he was able to escape.

Ginger clung to his t-shirt from behind, her bare feet making no noise whatsoever on the stone floor.

Chunks of rock began falling from the ceiling and smashing into the floor. Chace stifled a sneeze as dust tickled his nostrils. The wall beneath his palm was shaking harder, a sign they didn't have much time to escape.

Unable to see in the smoke, the griffin was able to smell them and was moving up and down the hallway, swinging its head left and right in an attempt to locate the two of them.

Chace breathed out as he made it around the corner at the intersection.

The griffin's head swung towards Chace, and he froze, reaching back to still Ginger's movements.

It lingered then swung away again.

Chace tugged her around the corner into the darker hallway, and they paused. The beast was between them and the entrance, a door he recalled being about ten meters away. The moment it opened, they'd be fair game for the griffin, which would have a chance to strike down Ginger before Chace was able to shift.

He leaned close to her to whisper against her ear, "Stay here. When I say, run. The door is straight this way."

"Chace, I –"

"Don't start with me, woman. I'm used to dealing with your stubborn daughter and will sling you over my shoulder."

She gave a sigh he took as acquiescence.

Chace moved away from her, towards the griffin. He crossed to the opposite side of the hallway then took a few steps towards the griffin. His dragon instincts picked up what his human senses weren't able to: the distance to the beast and what direction it was stealthily moving in. It had paced to the end of the hallway and was headed back towards Chace.

Chace whistled softly.

The creature froze a few feet away.

He whistled again.

The griffin bellowed a challenge and charged down the hallway.

Chace pressed his back to the stone wall and held out his foot. It smacked one of the griffin's forelegs, and the creature lurched forward. Before it caught its balance, Chace launched on top of its back.

The griffin went down with a squawk of fury.

Pebbles and dust rained down from the ceiling, and the sound of the hallway starting to collapse filled him with panic.

"Now!" Chace shouted. He wrapped his arms around the creature's neck and did his best to straddle the squirming body with his legs.

Ginger hurried by, her silent step undetectable but her movement on his dragon radar.

Chace struggled to hang onto the griffin. It flung him over its head then pounced.

Shit. Chace's arms went over his head to protect himself from the razor sharp beak of the griffin. It slashed through his forearms, sending hot pain through him. He kicked at the bulky body hovering over his.

The griffin retreated then snatched his arm with a clawed talon.

Light poured into the hallway as Ginger reached the exit and opened the door. The smoke was too thick to see more than her dark shape in the doorway before the door closed behind her.

The griffin lunged towards the door.

Chace snatched the leg nearest him, dragging the creature down to the ground. He bounced to his feet and launched over it towards the door, arms pumping hard.

The griffin slashed at him, its talons sinking into his back painfully. Chace stumbled and caught himself, dragon senses warning him about the creature's next move. Chace dived to the ground and rolled, smashing a kick into the beast charging him. Another swipe of the talons went through his chest, and he cursed, all too aware of the blood running down his body.

He bounded to his feet once more and forced his weakening body towards the door.

He slammed into the door, not expecting it to be so close. The griffin collided with him, pressing him to the cold metal.

Chace whirled and punched blindly then kicked. Both blows hit the creature, even if he wasn't certain where. It was enough to get it off his back so he could wrench the door open.

The moment he stepped foot into the brilliant midday outside, he began shifting. Chace threw his body weight against the door. It bucked open, and he shoved it closed.

"Ginger!" he grunted, his body shifting too quickly for him to control.

Ginger was a few feet away, scared gaze on the door. She darted forward at her name and braced herself against the door.

Chace staggered a few feet away to keep from squashing her when he transformed into a dragon. Fire flew through him, spurred by adrenaline and pain. He closed his eyes and focused hard, aware there were mere seconds between him becoming a dragon and a stupid griffin eating Skylar's mom.

"Chace!" her cry was alarmed.

Done. Chace whirled and saw Ginger on the ground, the bite-sized griffin getting ready to slash her.

With a bellow that made the rocks around them leap off the ground, Chace snapped the foul-scented griffin up in his powerful jaws and crushed it. The creature didn't have a chance to get a cry out before its body went limp and its blood filled his mouth.

He tossed it to the side, furious such a beast had managed to slash him up. Blood ran down his legs, chest and back.

The door leading into the mountain exploded outwards suddenly under the pressure of the explosion that caused the hallways to collapse. Chace flung up one wing, and the metal door deflected off him.

Dust and smoke poured out of the mountain. The rumbling slowed then stopped.

Relieved, Chace turned to make sure Skylar's mother was okay.

Ginger was trembling. Her bare feet were bloodied from the rocks. She shifted to pull her legs beneath her, gazing up at him in awe. She appeared younger than he expected, in her early thirties, not quite old enough to have a nineteen-year-old daughter. There were scars on her exposed limps, neck and down one side of her face, faded enough he hadn't been able to see them in the weak light of the vault.

It wasn't just the latest attempt to kill him that left him infuriated almost to the point where he wasn't able to think. The idea Ginger had been tortured, bled then frozen for six years dispelled any remaining inclination that Chace had about wanting to spare Freyja. He began to think everything she said was a lie, from blaming Dillon for killing hunters to turning over Ginger, once Chace succeeded in getting rid of her competition. Freyja had awoken his dragon magic a thousand years before but never told him what that meant or who he was supposed to be – the Protector's guardian. He knew now that she had probably always known, probably always been planning to use or kill him, once she found Skylar.

The next time he saw her, one of them wasn't walking away.

I did the right thing following her here, though. No part of him doubted it, even if Ginger was too taxed to go far. If he hadn't, would

Freyja have still dropped a mountain on Ginger? Rage filled him as he imagined what Ginger had gone through – what Freyja planned on putting Skylar through, if she caught her – and he almost felt relieved Gavin wasn't there to see what happened to the other half of his heart.

The rogue dragon would've gone crazy on sight.

Chace took a step towards her – and collapsed. He was bleeding heavily.

Ginger climbed to her feet with effort. "Others will come soon," she said urgently. "Can you shift back? I can cloak us more easily."

Chace stood and shook his head, not about to endanger them by remaining. Testing his wings, he hovered for a moment then moved forward, picking her up gently. Flying never caused this level of strain, and he knew he wasn't going far. Just far enough to find a safe place to hide.

He forced himself into the sky above the mountain, eyes roving the area below him for a safe spot. He didn't have the energy to fly for an hour and rendezvous with Skylar. All he needed was to find an area large enough for the cabin and then summon it.

His energy waning quickly, he wobbled in mid-flight, darkness beginning to creep into his mind. He spotted a valley between two peaks and descended quickly, barely preventing a hard landing. Releasing Ginger, he dropped then knelt.

Cabin! It was his last thought before his eyes closed, and unconsciousness claimed him.

Chapter Ten

"**M**Y GOD." SKYLAR GOT OUT of the SUV and stood frozen. She'd seen the smoke from the distance indicating there was a fire somewhere. The closer she drove to The Field, the more she prayed it wasn't what her instincts told her.

The bar that had acted as the shifters refuge was burned to the ground. She sensed a couple dozen living shifters scattered within the vicinity and just as many dead.

Her heart dropped to her feet at the sight of the damage.

What made Dillon turn against his own community to the point that he hunted and killed other shifters? She knew he was moody and difficult, but still … she never would've known he was capable of *this.*

Like I ever really knew any of them, she reminded herself. She'd had her own mind erased and foreign thoughts introduced, ones that told her it was okay to trust people like Dillon and Mason.

With a sidelong glance at the dark-skinned lion shifter approaching her, she couldn't dismiss the thought that he might still be lying to her.

"I didn't expect this," Mason stated, gaze on the destruction. "The shifters are scattered to the four winds now, aren't they?"

"Yeah, seems that way," she murmured. "Harder to form a revolt or support the rightful leadership if they're all over the world."

Skylar started forward, hoping to find Gunner. She sensed him nearby, along with a few more shifters. Was he, too, spooked? The man who stood up to Chace didn't seem like the kind to run.

She broke out into a jog, following her senses around the hill behind the ashes remaining of the bar.

Gunner was treating three wounded shifters under a lean-to, accompanied by another man she recognized as his and Chace's friend, a phoenix shifter named Luke.

"Gunner!" she called as she approached.

He stood and waited, hands on hips and features grim. His dark hair was pulled back, his muscular frame robed in clothing that appeared to have seen better days.

"What happened?" she demanded.

He rubbed his mouth before responding. "First Freyja then the griffins. They were pretty determined to scare us all away."

Her eyes fell to the three wounded shifters. One was in animal form – a massive white ape – while the other two were in human forms but unconscious.

"Is that Max?" she whispered, eyes on the snow-white ape whose hair was slashed with red.

"Yeah. Finally got his fight." Gunner eyed Mason. "Where's Chace?"

"We got separated," Skylar said. "He flew off. I'm not sure where." She did her best to keep her tone neutral and not to show any of her hurt or concern. She'd checked her phone a few times but not seen a text from him after the initial one where he said he was fine. "I should've stopped this."

"This isn't your fault," Gunner replied, softening.

"It *is*. My job is to protect you all. I just really … suck at it," she said in frustration.

"You're nineteen," Mason said in amusement. "Gunner here is close to seven hundred, and I'm fifteen hundred years old. If we weren't able to prevent this shit, what chance did you have?"

"You aren't a Protector!" she retorted. "I just … ugh! I don't know how to *be* all the different kinds of shifters I need to in order to stop this!"

"Easy, Sky," Gunner said. "Mason's right. You're learning. We all are. What we know: Freyja and Dillon need to be stopped before they hurt anyone else, and you can locate them so that we can do that."

She nodded, soothed by his simple wisdom. "I just wish Chace …" She clamped her mouth closed. "Wherever he is, I'm sure he's doing something that needs to be done." *But I really need you here, Chace!*

"We need a small army to take out Dillon and his griffins."

"There were about a hundred shifters here before we got chased off. I think about a quarter of them are still in the area," Gunner said. "We can round up those willing to help."

"And the dragons, when they wake up," she added. "This time, I'm not waiting for them to come to us. I can track every shifter in the universe, apparently, which means we can hunt them down one by one."

"I like that plan."

"I have one lasso," she said and pulled it from her pocket. "Even if it takes a week, we're going to put them into hibernation and end this!"

"Sounds like a plan. Will Chace be joining us soon?" Gunner asked a little too casually.

She heard what he didn't say, that it'd take more than the three of them to win this battle.

"I don't know," she murmured. "He went with Freyja somewhere."

Mason said nothing. Gunner frowned.

"I trust him," she said more confidently. "Whatever is going on, he's got a good reason for doing it."

"You don't want us to go after him?" Gunner asked.

She hesitated. She'd thought a few times about whether or not he was in trouble. "If I don't hear from him by tonight, then yes. Right now, I want to find Dillon and lasso the bastard."

"Dillon's a big bird to face without a dragon," Mason said, glancing at Gunner.

"I don't need backup," she reminded them. "If I get close enough, I can become something bigger than him. What I need is a ride to his location."

"*We* need a ride to his location," Mason corrected her. "Which means flying, right?"

She nodded. Gunner grumbled and Mason didn't appear pleased, but she knew they'd both be willing to go, despite their feline issues with flying.

"I can carry one," Luke said, stepping forward. With short blond hair and light eyes, he was tall and slender, lean in the way of a swimmer.

"You don't want to wait for Chace?" Mason asked again.

"He'll know where to find us." She smiled. "I've never seen a phoenix, Luke."

"All fire, no bite," Gunner replied.

Skylar smiled. A few hours ago, when Chace randomly disappeared, she'd figured he would return soon. The longer he was gone, however, the more concerned she became. While it was true he should be able to take care of himself, what happened if either he couldn't or wasn't willing to kill someone he'd been intimate with at some point?

What if he was in danger?

He'd gone off her radar an hour before, but he was alive. She felt his magic burning in her blood. His location had been far from Dillon's and no longer co-located with Freyja's. Uncertain how to interpret his absence when he wasn't close to either of the two people who posed a threat, she'd texted a few times then left it up to him.

His lack of response was as troubling as his sudden disappearance.

Trust him, Sky. It wasn't the first time she'd told herself this. It shouldn't be hard after their night together, but she was afraid of trusting anyone. People had a way of betraying or dying on her. *Not my dragon.*

"We got trouble," Mason growled, eyes on the sky. "Looks like the griffins are tracking you, Sky."

Her eyes flew up. She considered them. If one got close enough, she could turn into a griffin. But after her attempts at flying earlier, she knew how clumsy she was at it.

I can't be afraid to be who I am now, she told herself.

Luke was transforming into a phoenix nearby, and she glanced at him. While large, roughly the size of a small car, he wasn't anywhere near the size of a dragon. His head was the size of a human's, his plume of feathers the color of fire while the long, elegant tail of a phoenix smoldered.

"It's got to be easier to fly when I'm that size," she murmured and approached him.

Luke was a good two heads taller than her. She stopped close to him, listening for the senses that would separate his unique shifter signature from the others nearby. She keyed in on it.

"Mason, can you and Gunner find what army we can to face Dillon?" she asked, facing them. "I'm gonna give this flying thing a go again."

"You sure about that?" Mason asked.

"Yeah."

The griffins above had doubled in number.

"I'm tired of running," she decided. "At some point, I have to stop, right?"

"At the right time," Gunner agreed.

Ignoring him, she stripped out of her clothing, channeling the energy of a phoenix shifter.

"We'll see how this goes!" she said cheerfully. "I'm going after Dillon."

Gunner and Mason exchanged a look. She knew they were reluctant to act without Chace or the dragons, but she wasn't going to wait any longer to find Dillon after seeing the damage he'd done.

"We'll follow on foot," Gunner said finally. "Don't fly too fast. We need to be able to keep up."

Nodding, she closed her eyes and let the shifter magic take her.

Chapter Eleven

CHACE AWOKE WITH A GROAN, hating how badly his head was pounding. He lay still for a long moment to assess his body. Fear raced through him at the idea he was back on the beach again, unable to heal, waiting to die.

There was no pain, though, aside from his headache, only general body soreness and fatigue. He often felt this way after he'd healed. His body repaired itself automatically whenever he shifted but took time to replenish the blood loss, which was why his head throbbed.

"Glad you're awake," a quiet voice said.

It wasn't Skylar's, and it took him some thought to figure out whose it was. Chace opened one eye then the other. The sunlight streaming through the cabin's windows was too bright for his delicate head. He squinted.

"Pizza?" he asked, the scent tickling his nose.

"Your lair doesn't listen to me very well," Ginger said in some amusement. "But it did make you some food."

He pushed his body into a sitting position and leaned back against the headboard of his bed in the cozy cabin that was his home.

Ginger appeared a little healthier than before. There was color in her cheeks, and she wore clothing the cabin had probably found her. Her frame was too thin and frail for her slenderness to be natural, the circles under her eyes showing him how bad her experience had been.

Seated in the living area, she smiled, a cup of tea in her hands. Her gaze was direct and confident, if tired, her warm air cheerful, like Skylar's.

"What did they do to you?" he asked in a hushed voice.

She raised an eyebrow, another trait that reminded him of her daughter.

"Not that you look bad but ... well, you really do," he said.

"Just the usual. Interrogation, torture, shaved bald and bled near death." Her response was chipper. "It's all behind me, though."

"Why torture? I understand wanting your blood, but torture?"

"They needed to find Gavin and to know what Sky's gift was as well as mine," she answered. "I wouldn't tell them."

Chace didn't want to imagine the lengths someone like Dillon or Freyja were willing to go to in order to break Skylar's sweet mother. That Ginger had survived was nothing short of crazy.

"Freyja was in on it, too?" he asked.

"Of course. She's the brains. Dillon is the muscle. I wouldn't trust either of them for everything in the world. They argued a lot about how best to proceed with me and Skylar, but I don't have any doubt that they were both responsible for what happened."

"What about Mason?" he pressed. "Or do these questions bother you?" He searched her face, aware of how much suffering she'd gone through and unwilling to put her through more.

"No, I'm fine," she said with a faint smile. "I remember Mason. Briefly." She was pensive. "I met him when I first got there. I don't recall much else about him."

Chace said nothing, his thoughts on Skylar again. He wasn't able to shake the image of her ending up like Ginger. As powerful as Gavin was, he hadn't been able to protect his family, and Chace began to wonder what it'd take to safeguard his Sky.

Her skill was better suited to protecting her than Ginger's, once she learned to harness her magic and the different abilities each shifter gave her. He didn't want to think they'd always be in danger.

Which means Freyja and Dillon need to die. He also understood Skylar's view on killing, that it should only be done if necessary. She'd pleaded for the lives of those who helped brainwash her already.

Would she reconsider once she saw her mother? Would she realize there were certain shifters that just couldn't be allowed to live, if there was any hope for peace? It'd be different if Freyja hadn't been able to manipulate others from her hibernation.

Restless and worried, he flung off his comforter and wrapped his sheet around his waist then went to the bathroom. The cabin had clothing waiting, and he changed quickly.

"You're safe in the cabin," he said when he re-emerged. "You're in no shape to come with me."

Ginger flushed in anger.

"Don't even try," he warned, amused. "You're staying here. Cabin won't let you leave, even if you wanted to. I suggest you get some rest and regain your strength." *I couldn't save Gavin, but I will save you.*

"You're in no shape to fly," she said in irritation.

"I'll be fine," he assured her. "I've got to take care of some business, then I'll bring Skylar to meet you."

Ginger's expression softened. "I'd like that, Chace."

Uncertain how to respond to the amount of emotion in her voice, he nodded curtly. He went to the kitchenette and wolfed down pizza. It helped his pounding head, and he chugged two liters of water down before going to the door and looking out.

It was almost sunset. The dragons would be active soon. The fastest way to end this mess: convince them to wipe out those threatening the peace. Any thought he had about giving griffins mercy was gone with the realization of what would happen to Skylar, if he didn't act.

He'd go to the dragons for backup then rain down fire on those trying to hurt his Sky and destroy the shifter community.

"Your phone has been buzzing." Ginger's soft voice drew his attention from his planning.

Chace crossed to it, aware he probably had a few messages from Skylar already. He hadn't wanted to tell her what he was doing, in case Freyja was lying about Ginger. There were half a dozen messages from Sky and two from Gunner. He read through them quickly, frowning at Gunner's. Sky was asking where he was and if he was safe. Gunner, however, told him what she was doing.

For reals, dude. You need to be here. That girl is crazier than you. She's gonna challenge Dillon on her own.

"I've gotta get going," Chace mumbled and hurried out of the cabin. The last message from his friend was sent over an hour ago, while Chace had been unconscious.

He paused on the ledge outside the cabin, stretching his senses. Skylar was able to locate the shifters, but he didn't have the same skill. Instead, he sniffed the air, seeking the faintest scent of griffins. It didn't take much to assume that wherever they were, she'd be close, too.

He wasn't able to smell anything in his human form. With dragon senses that were a hundred times more powerful, he should be able to identify which direction to try at least.

He texted Skylar quickly. *Don't do anything crazy. I'm on my way.*

"Ginger, stay here!" he called over his shoulder once more. Willing the cabin to keep her safe, he undressed and shifted. *This mess ends tonight.*

Chapter Twelve

SOARING IN THE SKIES AS A phoenix wasn't much easier than a dragon. Skylar found her attention darting between keeping herself steady and eyeing the griffins, who didn't seem at all concerned about the smaller winged beasts in their midst. They were more occupied with trying to find *her*, circling and flying in dizzying circles without being able to locate her.

They don't know I'm a phoenix. Not for the first time, the idea of watching them flail around in confusion amused her.

Luke kept close to her, guiding them subtly further north without drawing the attention of the griffins. Far below, she was able to see the massive black lion and tan panther racing with ground eating strides in the same direction Skylar went. The flock of griffins was keeping pace with the creatures below, assuming what Dillon had about her being a panther shifter.

One of them snapped at her, and she squeaked involuntarily before steering away. At times, she found herself too interested in what was going on below to notice when she crossed over into the flight path of a cranky griffin. With her clothing strapped to her back, it was a little harder to balance.

Mason was right about me making a horrible Pegasus, she thought more than once. If a two-pound pack threw her off, what would a full-grown man riding her do to her ability to fly right?

She scoured the terrain below them. It had gone from the deserts of near The Field to the pine and mountains of the Tucson Mountains to the desert once more, headed west, towards California. They were closing in on Dillon's position, even if she wasn't certain where he was.

Dillon wasn't in the mountains. She wasn't certain why that surprised her, except that she half expected him to throw her off a cliff the next time they met. If a height loving griffin wasn't in the mountains, where was he? More importantly, *why?*

Another secret hideout? Freyja was there as well, which made her think it was a location the two didn't want discovered. Neither had moved since she began making her way there a couple of hours before.

The sun was perched on the horizon directly ahead of them, the sky beginning to turn vibrant shades of pinks and oranges. Skylar checked again to try to identify where Chace was.

He was hidden. How was that possible? Unease went through her, but she assumed, if he was in danger, it was at the hands of Dillon and Freyja, which meant she was headed the right way. She didn't doubt he was able to handle one of the shifters. Two, though, might be more of a challenge, especially if Dillon had another lasso or some other trickery up his sleeve.

She drifted out of the way of a large griffin, back towards Luke, and coasted for a moment on the sturdy wings of a phoenix. Flying was relaxing, when she wasn't worried about her balance or being sideswiped by a griffin. The cooling evening air ruffled her feathers. The stench of griffins was strong. Thus far, they were content to track the great cats below without making any attempt at snapping one of them up.

As she had a few times before over the flight, she tested the shifter magic to see if she was able to pick up the stream of griffin power. It was present, within reach, in case she needed to tap into it.

There. Skylar slowed her pace, her vision sharper as a phoenix than it had ever been as a human. She searched the area below her for some kind of structure or indication of where the two were hiding.

Nothing was below them, aside from the open desert.

Puzzled, she precariously inched closer to Luke, leery of letting one of his wings knock her off kilter, and nipped at his tail feathers.

He spun in mid air, mouth open as if to spew fire at the griffin that dared touch the magnificent plume trailing him. When he saw her, he closed his mouth and hovered, waiting.

Skylar looked down emphatically at the area below them.

The griffins slowed when the cats below them began walking, and the milling creatures around her scared her for a moment. She feared any nudge or accidental brush of her wings that might send her toppling towards the ground. Easing away from the griffins, she awkwardly began drifting towards the ground. With some apprehension, she managed to land near the great cats.

Luke alighted beside her, and Mason grumbled loudly before stopping in front of them.

Not yet convinced she was in the right spot, Skylar paced on all fours to where she sensed the two then scratched at the ground beneath her.

Her talons scraped metal, and she cringed at the sound of nails on chalkboard.

There's something beneath here. Skylar urged her body to change quickly and braced herself for the pain of transforming into a human once more. A moment later, she pulled on her clothing then dropped to her knees beside the spot, lasso in hand.

"They're here," she said.

A glance at the sky revealed the griffins still swarming around. They didn't seem alarmed she was there and kept their distance, making her pause.

What were they up to? Why weren't they attacking their boss's number one enemy?

Unless Dillon wants me to find him.

Skylar leaned back and assessed the area around her. Whatever facility was beneath the desert sand, it was well hidden. There was no doubt that Freyja and Dillon were both beneath her feet and no doubt she had no idea how to get to where they were.

"Hey, Mason," she called and waved the great cat over.

She stood, wanting to ask if he knew of this hiding place from having worked with the two before. Trotting towards him, she felt the ground lurch beneath her.

Skylar landed on her knees and looked down, startled. The glimmer of metal was dim in the indirect rays of light from the setting sun, but the shift in the ground was enough to show her the extent of the structure she stood on. It was a good twenty meters by twenty meters.

Climbing to her feet, she took a step to test the ground beneath her. Assured it was safe once more, she started forward.

Mason's roar warned her a second too late.

The earth beneath her gave out, and Skylar fell.

Shift! Was it her mind or someone yelling at her? Her instincts were too scattered for her to choose any one shifter's signature to transform into, and she tumbled helplessly into the darkness, unable to gauge how far away the ground was or what waited for her.

The lasso flew free, topping with her into the darkness. She hit the ground a second later and heard the sickening snap of her leg.

Skylar groaned. Lights exploded in her mind, along with a flare of hot pain that streaked up her shin into the rest of her.

Fuck that hurt! She lay still for a moment, breathless from the impact and sensations in her right leg. It was broken, which made her plan of facing Dillon a little trickier than she expected.

The sound of padded feet hitting shale a few feet away told her she hadn't been the only one to fall. She sensed Mason padding towards her. His warm breath tickled her neck a moment before his soft muzzle nudged her.

"I'm … okay," she said, pushing his massive head away. *Mostly.*

He gripped her by her collar and hauled her up. Skylar elevated her right leg to prevent any part of it from touching the ground, hissing at the pain caused by the movement. She flung an arm over his back and rested her weight on him, fighting back the sensation that she was going to pass out or throw up.

"Shit. Dropped the lasso," she muttered. Unable to see in the dark, she had no way of finding it. "Where are we?" A glance upward revealed the dying light from the way they'd fallen. It was a good ten meters high, and her voice echoed around them. The darkness smelled wet while the sound of a gurgling stream came from nearby. The ground beneath her had been rocky, natural terrain.

Not a compound, she realized, taking in the dark world. *Cavern.*

Southern Arizona was littered with hidden caverns and sunken rivers. As her eyes adjusted, she became aware of the faint glow of fluorescent rocks lining distant cave walls.

The sound of metal grating on rock came from above. Skylar watched with concern as the skylight to the rest of the world closed slowly, sealing her in the darkness.

Her phone vibrated, and she pulled it free, relieved to see a note from Chace.

Don't do anything crazy. I'm on my way. She read it silently then smiled. "Too late, dragon." Tucking the phone away, she shivered in the damp chill of the underground cave. Mason was warm and solid beside her.

She looked around to distract herself then tested her shifter radar to find Freyja and Dillon.

"They're here, Mason," she whispered. Her senses told her nothing more, aside from the fact she was practically on top of Dillon and within meters of Freyja. She could pick up both of their shifter signatures, a sign of how close they really were.

Yet she didn't see or hear anyone.

Mason growled, and she guessed he was able to identify what her human senses couldn't. Skylar took a deep breath. She'd ventured this far to fix the issue of them hurting shifters once and for all. She wasn't going to back down now, and she judged she had a short time before her leg put her into shock.

"Dillon, Freyja, I came to talk," she called firmly. "We need to settle this once and for all."

With the exception of Mason's growling, she heard no other shifter.

"I don't want any other shifters or humans getting hurt," Skylar said. "I'm sure we can come to some kind of agreement."

"Agreement." It was Dillon's voice, closer than she expected. "The way I see it, you're in our backyard. You're hurt and ten meters below ground, without your dragon. What motivation do I have to *negotiate* with you?"

Good point. "Can I ask you something, Dillon? As an old friend?" she returned, mind working quickly on how to counter his challenge.

He was silent.

"If I had my dragon with me and an army of shifters at my back, would you be willing to negotiate then?"

"No."

She shouldn't feel bad knowing Chace was right about him, but she did. Maybe it was her desire to preserve as much life as possible, or maybe it was the last remnants of the relationship she'd once had with Dillon. But no part of her wanted to kill him, even if that was what was best for the shifter community as a whole.

"Well," she said, taking a deep breath. "I figure you all have wanted something from me since the beginning. I'll trade you whatever that is for the safety of the shifters."

Another long quiet, then Freyja spoke.

"Smart," she said. Her voice came from the opposite direction of Dillon's. "What makes you think we still want anything from you?"

"I'm not dead," Skylar said simply. She tested the shifter magic again to determine who was closer. "Dillon may not be interested, but you're a whole lot smarter than him, Freyja. What do you think of my deal?"

"I think it's worth a listen," the dragon shifter stated. "Though I have no real need to negotiate, either. Chace is buried under a mountain, which means it's just Mason between you and me. Not much of a challenge, is it?"

"People love to tell me they've gotten rid of my dragon," Skylar said in some amusement. While she wasn't able to sense him, she knew he wasn't dead after the text. "Never seems to work that way. But, if you want me in exchange for keeping all the other shifters safe, I'm happy to talk to you."

"No deal," Dillon spat. "We'll take what we want from you! There's nothing you can do to stop us, Skylar."

"Now, Dillon, let her talk." Freyja sounded closer.

Skylar squinted but wasn't able to make out anything in the utter darkness of the cave. They were too far for the faint glimmer of fluorescent rocks to be of use, and her senses were too dulled to help her.

"You'd walk away with me right now? Do whatever I tell you?" Freyja continued.

Mason snapped at her.

Skylar strained to hear the movement of the shifters stalking them before finally giving up. She needed to be a dragon or lion to know where they were.

"It's not part of the plan," Dillon snapped. "We don't need her to come voluntarily. We just need her chained to a wall somewhere."

"For what purpose?" Skylar ventured.

"Locating the shifters. Controlling them in a way only you can. I don't know what your gift is, but we'll figure it out fast," Freyja replied. "Dillon, our goal has always been to help the shifter community retain a strong, deserving leader. We might get what we want in every way this way."

"Strong leader," Skylar repeated. "You or Dillon?"

"Me, of course."

Dillon snorted.

"Dillon *is* bigger, stronger physically," Skylar mused. "And the dragons won't follow you, Freyja, once they realize you turned on them."

"Dragons will fall in line behind the strongest of their kind, like griffins. It's how it's always worked," Freyja said dismissively. "Dillon doesn't have the mental capacity to lead."

"*I* don't?" Dillon snarled. "Who manipulated everything while you were in hibernation? I delivered Sky and the others on a silver platter!"

"And killed off a bunch of shifters to renew the dragon-griffin divide in the community," Skylar added. "Then again, Freyja hasn't exactly inspired anyone to follow her either by selling out everyone who has ever done business with her. Does that bother you, Dillon? Or do you think you're safe from being sold out?"

Silence.

Mason nudged her, as if to hush her. He was probably right. Provoking both her enemies at once, when she had a game leg and minimal backup, was probably not the smartest strategy.

Or was she talking so much because she'd started to slide into shock?

"You never did tell me what happened to my mother," she voiced. "I think I deserve to know that much, after all you've both done to fuck with my life."

"Dead," Freyja said flatly. "Now, onto business."

Skylar's heart sank. She knew as much, but hearing the confirmation from the person who probably had a hand in her mother's death made it somehow more final. She was having trouble focusing at the moment. The pain in her leg had gone from fiery to numb and she shivered, uncertain if she was hot or cold.

Shit. She needed to do something quickly to get medical treatment or at least, to get out of this horrible darkness, where she was at their mercy.

She tested the magic again. Freyja was speaking, but Skylar struggled to focus on her words. There was a chance she could escape by flying upwards towards the top of the cavern, where she'd fallen through. Or maybe even defend herself. She could set something on fire to see what was going on …

Shaking her head, Skylar forced her attention back where it

belonged.

"… your deal," Freyja was saying.

"Could you repeat that?" Skylar asked.

There was a sigh. "I said, I'm willing to consider your deal, if you're serious about it."

"You won't let Dillon hurt any other shifters?" Skylar asked. "And you'll let Mason go?"

"I won't let Dillon hurt anyone else, including Mason."

Skylar frowned. No part of her believed for a moment that Freyja was willing to spare the shifters, not after all the dragon shifter had done to manipulate her way to where she wanted to be.

"You hear that, Dillon? You're not *allowed* to hurt anyone," Skylar prodded. "Kinda sucks taking orders after you've been running things the past thirteen years or so."

"Look, girl, whatever you're doing, it's not –" Freyja started.

"No, she's right," Dillon responded. "Why should I listen to you, Freyja? The griffins are mine. We've done all your grunt work. What do you bring to the table?"

Tension between the two allies ratcheted up another notch. Skylar didn't know what was holding the two together. Dillon and Freyja were mismatched in every way she could imagine, and both were selfish beyond imagination. If she took their common enemy out of the equation, would their tenuous relationship fall to pieces?

"The master plan, maybe?" Freyja shot back. "This isn't about us, Dillon. We both need *her.*"

"Whoever wants to control the shifters needs me," Skylar noted. "So then whoever has me, does he or she win by default?"

"Stop it, girl," Freyja snapped. "We've agreed to your deal. I assume that means you'll leave quietly with us."

"Sure," Skylar said cheerfully. She hopped forward. The jolting movement renewed the pain in her leg. "Shit."

Mason shifted towards her, supporting more of her body weight as she sagged. A wave of dizziness washed over her.

"Give me a minute," she said. She looked upward into the inky blackness again. If she were having trouble standing on two feet, would she be as hindered on four? "Are we going up or out a different way?"

"Different way," Dillon replied. "Back way, where anything can happen."

Skylar smiled to herself. "Thank god you both need me alive or I might be worried. Wonder if it's the same for the two of you?" She was shivering. Shock was setting in, which meant, if she planned on escaping, she was short on time.

Mason hadn't stopped rumbling from deep within his chest since the first one of them spoke. Skylar rested against him for a moment.

"I need to shift," she whispered. "Dragon, griffin or cat?"

He tossed his mane.

"Sky, come on," Dillon said impatiently.

"I'm having a small problem walking."

"How bad?"

She tested her leg and quickly took the weight off it. Pain shot through her. "Bad," she said through gritted teeth.

"Give her a hand, Dillon," Freyja snapped. "Mason, you go your own way with no incident and I'll respect my promise to Skylar."

Mason roared in response.

"Do it," Skylar said, burying both her hands in his thick mane. She leaned closer. "Bring Chace back with you."

The great lion growled loudly.

"Come get me, Dillon," Skylar said.

She heard his step on the shale around her. A moment later, his arm wrapped around her. She released Mason, praying her tiny semblance of a plan worked.

"Hurry up, Dillon," Freyja called. Without hearing her leave, Skylar was able to determine the woman was a good twenty meters away just by her voice.

"She doesn't cut you any slack, does she?" Skylar murmured to Dillon, grimacing when they took their first step.

"Shut up, Sky."

"No, really, Dillon. I've never known you to –"

"Listen." He whirled her and gripped both arms hard. "Whatever you're doing, it won't work. You fucked up if you think I'm gonna let her keep me from doing what I need to with the community! You turned yourself in and will get a front row seat to what I'm planning!"

You're a real dick, Dillon. Skylar struggled to keep her balance.

"What exactly do you want to do with me?" she asked. "What good is a Protector to you?"

"We'll find out when we know what your gift is," he replied. He started forward again, this time yanking her by the arm. "It's gotta be more than you being able to turn into a stupid cat."

Her injured leg exploded into pain the moment she put pressure on the ball of her foot. "Oh, god!" she gasped. The lights reappeared in her mind, driving her towards unconsciousness.

Dillon muttered a curse then stopped, slinging her over his shoulder.

Skylar fell into the in-between place for a long moment before biting her lip hard. The sudden burst of pain pulled her back.

"So …" She tried hard to focus on her words. "If you take Protectors to use their magic … what did you want from my mother?"

"Her gift. She had the ability to hide things. Compounds, shifters, whatever."

The claim startled her. Suddenly, the slayers operations – and the shifters' inability to sense or escape them – crystalized. "And that's why Gavin didn't know about the slayers. No one did," she said in surprise. She tried to maneuver her injured leg into not bobbing against his chest with every step he took. "Brilliant."

"We built an operation under the noses of every shifter in existence," he replied. "They never saw us coming."

Wow. Her mother was a badass, if she could hide so much activity, even from those who were caught in the middle of it. "So how did that work? You took her magic?" she asked.

"Not exactly. Magic is in the blood. We took her blood. Used it to shield the compounds and even to brainwash you."

His words made Skylar even more nauseated. They'd drained her mother of blood! How sick was that? Was that what they planned to do to her, too?

"But how could you do that for so long if ..." *she wasn't alive?* She stopped, stunned by her own realization. "She was alive the whole time, wasn't she?"

"Was, yeah." Dillon sounded smug. "Didn't need her after *you* blew the lid off our operation."

Guilt flooded her. Skylar's eyes watered as much from the pain in her leg as the feeling of her heart breaking. If she had known the cost of bucking the system ... if she'd had some small clue that her mother's life was at risk ...

"You're a bastard, Dillon," she whispered.

"We're even now."

"I didn't kill Caleb!" She all but shouted. "And you killed two of my parents!"

"Freyja killed your mother this morning. I had nothing to do with it."

Skylar's breath caught, and her chest seized so quickly, she couldn't breathe.

This morning. She'd been searching for her mother for years, only to miss saving her by a few hours? It was beyond her ability to imagine how close she'd been and how badly she'd failed.

"That shut you up. Now, listen to me, Sky," Dillon said, his voice growing hushed. "Freyja killed your mother in cold blood. Your father died in battle. You've got no chance, if you take her side. You know what I'm capable of if you cross me. Why don't we make our own deal now?"

Skylar listened, barely registering the words. After the blow Dillon just gave her, she wasn't certain what to think or even if she could believe him. But the idea her mother had been alive until only a few hours ago ...

"Come with me, and I won't fuck you up."

"Is that the best you've got?" she asked with a strangled laugh.

"It's all you're getting," he retorted. He stopped walking. "Right now, I can do unspeakable things to you, Sky. We're twenty meters underground. There's no one to save you."

Except for me. She said nothing, not about to let her little secret slip. Even if she did shift, she'd be too clumsy to know how to defeat him. She might be able to fight him off long enough to escape, though, which made her secret even more valuable.

He was doing what she wanted – severing from Freyja. If the two of them ever went into battle, she doubted either would survive.

Especially not once Chace got there. And he would. This time, she wouldn't doubt him. He'd leapt off a cliff to prove himself, and she believed in him.

"Sure, why not?" she mumbled. She was feeling hot, starting to overheat. Her skin was clammy, and her leg was fluctuating between numbness and agony. "Not to alarm you, but I'm about to get sick."

"Don't you dare!" Dillon snarled. He began walking again, this time faster.

How was I ever half in love with this jackass? Skylar swallowed hard, lightheaded.

"What can you do as a Protector?" he asked tersely. "Or do I have to figure it out?"

"It's hard to explain."

"So you do know?"

"Yeah. But right now ..." she drifted off and coughed.

"Fuck, Sky, if you throw up on me ..." Dillon set her down none too gently.

Skylar sucked in a deep breath, willing herself not to throw up. The urge subsided, and she wiped the tears off her face.

"My leg is broken," she groaned. "How far are we going?"

Dillon said nothing. He rested a hand on her forehead then shifted away.

"Where did Freyja go?"

"None of your business."

"If you don't know, do you really think you should trust her out of your sight? I mean, she could be meeting with the dragons to take you out. It's almost dark."

"Stop it, Sky!"

She sagged, a chill running through her.

Dillon was silent.

Skylar stretched down to touch her injured leg and cursed when she felt the shinbone nearly protruding through her skin.

"If you need to go ... handle something ... I'm not going anywhere," she told him.

There was another pause, then a reluctant, "Stay here. If you move a fucking inch, I will kill all your precious shifters."

Skylar said nothing. She didn't hear him leave and waited.

"Dillon?" she whispered into the darkness.

The sound of a heavy metal door closing a short distance away was the only response.

"Oh, god." She breathed out hard, her body hurting. Using her upper body strength, Skylar lifted herself on top of an uncomfortable boulder.

Try to make it on two legs or shift into something else and see if four legs worked better?

She peeled off her shirt and tossed it then decided saving her clothing wasn't worth the pain of moving her hurt leg. Instead she steadied her breathing, closed her eyes, and pulled in the magic of the closest shifter she could.

Damn griffin. It was Dillon's signature with Freyja's being the next closest.

Skylar focused on Dillon and drawing his magic into her body. She was almost too fevered and numb to notice the pain of her body being torn a part and rebuilt. When the transformation was finished, she tested herself.

Her right back leg was useless, but she had the use of her others, which stabilized her body. She didn't feel the overwhelming need to vomit or lie down, as if one bad leg wasn't as cumbersome to a creature with four as it was to one with two. She was still, growing accustomed to the senses of a griffin. She was able to see shapes and a pathway in the darkness that had befuddled her before, along with the ability to hear the sounds coming from the door through which Dillon had gone as well as from the spot where she fell into the cavern in the first place. The trickling stream came off as a roar now, and she was able to smell moss growing on the walls and the chalky scent of rocks.

The section of the cavern where she stood now was too narrow to spread her wings. She turned and hobbled on three legs back to the expansive cabin, now able to see what she couldn't before. The gaping underground cave was large enough for her and Chace to stand wing-to-wing without reaching each side. Her sharp vision was able to see the lines of sky between the heavy metal sheets lying over top of the cavern.

Waiting for Dillon to return and finish her off wasn't an option.

Skylar spread her wings, judging their weight and what it'd take to balance once she was in the air. She lifted and lowered once, pulling herself off the ground. While her head hurt from the injured leg, she almost roared in relief at easing the pressure by being off the ground. She moved her wings carefully and hovered awkwardly.

The griffins wings were half the size of a dragon's – but sturdier, thicker. They felt more like what she expected them to, not like the translucent, delicate wings of a dragon.

When confident she was able to balance in the air, she propelled herself upward, using her animal senses to gauge her distance from the top. When she was close, she lowered her head and neck and attempted to slam her shoulder into it.

Her first strike was off, and she toppled backwards. Catching her large body with her wings, she evaluated briefly then tried again.

Why can't I just know *how to be whatever shifter I am?* She groaned internally. Each beast was like learning her body over again. While she was acclimating faster, she didn't yet feel comfortable flying or walking on four legs. There was a level of instinctive coordination the other shifters appeared to have naturally, whereas she struggled to adapt.

Skylar smashed into the metal ceiling twice more until managing to push aside two sheets of metal to reveal a crack about a foot wide. It wasn't large enough for her to push through. She glanced towards her tail, recalling how Dillon had used his to wrap around her neck and fling her around.

With more patience than she thought possible, she ordered the tail to push through the crack and widen it. If wings were a challenge, a tail was like trying to order around a body part that belonged to someone else.

Her keen senses picked up on the metal door opening deep within the cavern. It didn't take seeing who was there for her to guess Dillon was on his way back for her.

Come on, tail! Skylar growled aloud and pushed at the metal. One gave with a grating sound she knew was going to be audible to a griffin like Dillon. Panicking at the thought of facing him in the confines of the cavern, she pushed harder, finally managing to shove open a large enough space for her to ram through.

Skylar heard the sounds of breaking bones that indicated Dillon was rapidly transforming into his griffin form and squawked more loudly than she intended. She rocketed upward, smashing through the metal sheets. One flipped over while the other grated against stone as it moved.

She drew a deep breath and vaulted into the sky. With some surprise, she smacked into another body in the air above the desert and tumbled back towards the ground. Skylar flailed, her wings ballooning out to catch her. Steadying herself, she took a moment to look around.

Dragons. They were everywhere, their different colored scales glowing faintly in the starlight. Unable to tap into her Protector GPS when she was in flight, she spun to see who was there, looking for Chace.

A squawking roar from below drew her focus. She saw the furious ball of feathers and fur barreling towards her, out of the cavern.

Shit. Skylar flew upwards, ignoring the dragons, until one of them lunged at her. It dawned on her they thought *she* was the enemy. Skirting away from the dragon taking too keen of an interest in her, she found her path on a collision course with Dillon, whose mastery of flight and hunting his prey far outweighed her ability to escape.

She turned tail and soared away, not caring where she went. The other dragons began circling, and she sensed them change directions to attack the two massive griffins in their midst.

Cursing Dillon and everyone under the sun, Skylar pulled at the nearest thread of magic, that of the dragon chasing her, and ordered her body to shift.

Pain rippled through her. It wasn't the pain of shifting but of a dragon trying to sear off one wing. The feathers burst into flame, and she plummeted towards the earth.

Shift, shift, shift! She closed her eyes and fell. Her body tore itself a part and transformed mid-flight into that of a dragon.

The pain in her wing extinguished as her body absorbed the flames. Fire blazed through her, and she heard the roars of those pursuing.

Skylar unleashed the longer, more delicate wings of a dragon and caught herself a few feet from the ground. Her senses picked up those near here, the dragons that had stopped pursuing in confusion, while Dillon fought free of two to charge after her.

The griffin smashed into her, his talons shredding one wing and clawing a chunk out of her side. Skylar's scream came out as a furious bellow. She and Dillon hit the ground and rolled, his beak and talons tearing into her. She coughed flames at him and shoved him with her good legs, digging her claws into his body to help her balance.

They rolled to a stop. Skylar's breathing was labored, pain in her side and down one leg. Her injured wing hurt too, and vaguely, she wondered what part of her human body would reflect the damage once she transformed. No longer distracted by the need to concentrate on flying, she watched Dillon recover with one eye while seeking out any other animal she was able to find. Her wings were useless, and she wasn't going to be able to hide easily when she was the size of an SUV and weighed a metric ton.

Dragons and griffins. They were the closest. Farther away, she sensed feline shifters and at least one wolf. Skylar considered her options. She needed the ability to run fast and maneuver.

Dillon staggered to his feet and shook out his short, thick mane.

Skylar stretched for the magic of a mountain cat, the smallest of the felines she found within a few kilometers of the cavern. Holding her breath, she willed herself to shift. Her bones cracked in response to her silent commands. Her muscles and skin tightened, her body imploding to create a creature whose shoulders were no more than half a meter off the ground.

She tested her body. Her leg was still injured but the pain from the wounds in her sides had dulled, as if shifting made her heal some of her injuries. Her right front shoulder felt as if it had been bruised, and she guessed that was the remains of Dillon shredding her wing.

Without waiting for Dillon to figure out what was going on, she bounded away, darting quickly into the darkness. Skirting boulders and cacti, she used the feline's night vision to guide her. She'd caught a glimpse of a gaggle of shifters – including Chace – about two kilometers away, behind a few hills.

Dragons attacked Dillon, distracting him, while one of the great beasts hovered over her, as if trying to figure out what was going on with the creature that shifted from griffin to dragon to feline within minutes.

She glanced up at the dragon coasting overhead.

Did he sense the Protector but not understand what was happening? She wasn't certain why he wasn't attacking.

Dillon, however, was under bombardment. Squawking, roaring and fire all came from behind her as he fought the dragons to get to her. She skirted a hill and paused to look back.

He was holding his own a little too well. The sight of a dragon going down beneath his claws terrified her. Her Protector radar told her that the dragon was dead, a moment before its body burst into fire.

At his max with the meddling dragons, the griffin glared in her direction then turned and ran, leaping into the black hole back into the cavern.

Skylar gave a full body shake and sat for a moment, her hind leg hurting badly. She was panting, her breathing labored from her achy, tight ribs and the effort of shifting. She needed a nap and some food, two things she suspected she wasn't going to find this night.

Wounded and beat, Skylar got to her three working feet and began at a limping trot towards Chace. The dragons above left her alone, circling lazily as they followed, and occasionally diving close enough for her to smack a wing.

Her pace slowed after a mile, the strain of her evening wearing on her. The sand was soft beneath her paws, the desert breeze filled with too many wonderful scents for her to identify. She caught a whiff of Chace's honey-bonfire smell and shivered, loving its richness even more in animal form.

Lost in exhausted thought, she didn't register the clicking of her nails on metal until she'd walked a few feet onto the hidden metal sheets.

Skylar froze, ears flickering back and forth, and stared at her feet, struggling to register what she was stepping on. With her nocturnal senses, she was able to see how far it extended and also that there was a gap between two sheets that extended for about a meter.

She sniffed the wind, and the faint scent that returned made her take a few steps back.

Griffin.

Skylar hurried off the metal plates, refocusing on her Protector radar. She almost gave a cry of frustration and scolded herself for losing track of such dangerous enemies.

It wasn't just Dillon below her, but Freyja, too.

This isn't good. If she shifted into a dragon again, would she be healed or would the wounds Dillon caused reappear?

The dragons were circling above, and she was still a kilometer out from Chace. Did she make a run for it or tiptoe by and hope the two below weren't lying in wait for her? After a split hesitation, she skirted the metal covering entrances to the caverns below and broke into a trot.

If she was able to sense them, they were more than capable of identifying her as well. At the sudden thought, she began loping.

No sooner had she cleared the caverns than the sound of metal grating against stone reached her. Skylar looked over her shoulder. Starlight glimmered off the translucent wings of the silver-white dragon emerging from the depths of the underground cave. For a moment, the ethereal beauty of the large dragon left her mesmerized.

Until the familiar gaze settled on her.

Skylar turned and ran, not about to become dinner for the dragon that allegedly killed her mother.

The dragons far above didn't seem interested in Freyja, as if they either didn't know what she'd done, or like she claimed, they didn't care enough to mess with a stronger dragon.

Skylar ran, too aware of the danger lurking overhead.

Freyja took flight and soared above her before diving, tucking her wings to compel her as fast as possible.

Skylar assessed the shifters she had access to for something a bit bigger, able to withstand the attack of a furious dragon. After a moment, she hunched down on the ground and transformed from the tiny bobcat into something much more likely to cause damage.

Mason's lion. The size of a small car, Skylar's talons were longer than her fingers and her teeth sharp enough to cut through a dragon wing. She waited until Freyja was close enough then launched upwards, clearing the ground by three meters, even with the wounded leg. Skylar slashed at the shimmering wing nearest her and felt it slide through her paws, until she engaged her talons.

Freyja roared.

Skylar used her body weight and yanked backwards, dragging the dragon to the ground, the way she'd seen Mason do. Freyja crashed down, bellowing angrily.

Skylar released her and stood back, snarling and growling at the white dragon. She had no idea whether she could believe Dillon's words about Freyja killing her mother, but she didn't doubt Freyja had committed enough evil any way she looked at it, no matter whose lives were involved.

Freyja shook out her wings. The one Skylar grabbed wouldn't fold, a sign the thin bones were broken.

Satisfied, Skylar crouched down and waited for the dragon to make the next move.

Freyja eyed her, smoke curling out of her nostrils.

Skylar sensed Dillon before the griffin emerged from the cavern. He alighted behind her, and she shifted to see both of them.

Come on, dragons! She glanced upwards. They'd started to grow near as soon as Dillon appeared, though more cautious this time.

Freyja inched closer.

Skylar snapped at her. She had a better chance of defending herself as a shifter, but the odds were looking bleaker by the moment.

Dillon's tail rose up as he prepared to use it to grab her. It snaked towards her. She batted down the first strike then snapped its tip off with the second.

Griffins taste worse than they smell. Spitting out the bit of tail, she waited for him to attack once more.

The whip-like appendage snapped towards her, this time headed for one of her feet rather than her neck. Skylar danced away, twisting to avoid the too-smart tail. Smacking it down, she trapped it beneath her large paws. Just as she was about to snap it up in her mouth, the familiar sensation of claws wrapping around her midsection distracted her.

She was yanked off the ground and hauled into the air at breakneck speed, fast enough that she almost lost consciousness. To make it worse, Freyja was squeezing her hard enough that she wasn't able to breathe.

I can't shift! Skylar watched the ground grow farther away quickly. Unable to catch her breath or maneuver in the dragon's clutches, she was helpless, unless Freyja dropped her, giving her time to shift.

The higher they went, the harder it was for her to breathe. The atmosphere was thinning too much. Blackness edged her vision, and she roared in frustration, the bellow ringing off the canyon below. Her body sagged, and tunnel vision formed.

Skylar fell unconscious.

Chapter Thirteen

"**YOU SAID SHE'S HERE?**" Chace paced, sensing Skylar nearby without seeing her. He peered into the night sky at the dragons circling the area.

"Yeah." Mason's chest was heaving. "Underground. There are huge … caverns."

Chace looked down at his feet with new concern. They'd been scouring the skies and ground for her. Every shifter was able to track her, yet when they went to her location, no one was there. He'd never thought to look for a griffin and dragon underground.

"Why the fuck did you leave her?" He turned on the half-dressed lion shifter.

Mason straightened. "She told me to find you. I think she was stalling them."

She knows I'm here. Chace yanked off his shirt to shift.

Skylar was in trouble, if she was with Dillon and Freyja. Too clumsy as a shifter to fight a veteran like Dillon, she was also the most capable of escaping that he knew. She'd find a way, if there were one.

If not, I'll fuck that place up to get to you.

The roar of an angry creature split the quiet, and he froze, eyes on the sky once more.

"That sounds like a lion," Gunner said from beside them.

"Lions don't fly," Mason said, following his gaze.

I'm coming for you, Sky. Chance ripped off his clothes, taking off at a run in the direction of the sound. Shifting forced him onto all fours, and he scampered forward as his body changed. Within seconds, the pain and reorganization of his insides ceased, and he leapt into the sky.

His sense of smell found her before his eyes did. She was the only lion in the world that would smell like a combination of peach shampoo and fur.

Freyja was easy to spot, her white body and wings standing out like the moon far above. Clutched in her talons was a great cat Chace knew to be Skylar. He soared upward, his powerful wings beating hard, his weakness forgotten at the idea of Freyja hurting Skylar. He closed the distance between them quickly. Any question he had about why Skylar hadn't turned into a dragon and flown away stopped when he saw the limp form of the lioness.

Rage filled him with dragon fire hotter than any he'd ever experienced. Not only had Freyja manipulated everyone for the past two decades to get to Skylar and her mother, but she was also about to kill Skylar, if she went much higher.

Chace bellowed a warning to the mastermind behind the slayers and The Field.

Freyja glanced down then renewed her effort to climb into the heavens. Dragons had no problem handling the thinned atmosphere at higher altitudes, but Skylar would be lucky if all that happened to her was a coma.

He didn't know what the dragon was doing. If Skylar's blood was the key to Freyja ruling the shifters, she was risking a lot by pulling a non-dragon this far into the atmosphere. He guessed she initially meant to knock out Skylar, so the shifter queen couldn't transform and flee, and then freaked out when she saw Chace pursuing her.

Chace bellowed once more.

Freyja ignored him.

Grimly, he realized that there would be no peaceful way to end this. Carefully planning how to disable Freyja without hurting Skylar, he drew abreast of the white dragon and slowed his speed to match hers.

She spewed fire at him to try to distract him then darted away, tucking her wings to start a rapid free fall.

Chace wasn't about to flinch now, not when Skylar's life depended on him. He effortlessly adjusted to Freyja's new course, taking in the grip she had around Skylar. She'd drop Skylar if she were unconscious or dead. He didn't see her letting go voluntarily.

Cold wind raced by his ears, chilling his muzzle. He maneuvered closer to Freyja carefully, unwilling to look down at how far he had until he had to unleash his wings. He'd seen Gavin fall like this with Skylar in his arms and not get up; he'd do the same, if it came to it. He was going to end whatever dangerous game Freyja was playing for good.

When he was close enough to the white dragon, Chace pulled back his lips and bared his long fangs. He gripped Freyja's body with his claws to keep her steady then sank his teeth deep into her neck.

Blood sprayed into his mouth at the lethal bite. The human side of him was disgusted, the animal side clamoring for more.

Freyja screeched and tried to fling him off, tossing her body left and right to destabilize him.

Chace released her with his mouth, still holding her in place with his talons. Blood splattered him as she began to bleed out. Freyja hemorrhaged blood. It coated his face and neck, the warmth traveling down his chest and forelegs as well.

Waiting until her struggling grew weaker, he bit her again then unfurled his wings to catch them. The weight of two dragons and a lioness was enough to cause his weakened body strain, and he quickly realized that – while he could slow their fall – he wasn't going to be able to keep them from hitting the ground.

Freyja was getting weaker fast. One of her wings drifted away from her body as she began to lose control, sending them somersaulting towards the earth,

Chace released her neck and clawed at her body, not about to risk losing his grip on the out of control dragon. He maneuvered her around until he was able to reach her leg with his mouth. Without a second thought, he snapped one of the legs holding Skylar in two.

Freyja's bellow was softer, fading with her life. She reflexively let go of Skylar.

Chace shoved away from the dragon and righted himself midair. No longer concerned with Freyja, his sole focus became catching Skylar and preventing them both from hitting the ground. He dived after the falling lioness and swept her heavy frame up with all four legs. Skimming a plateau, he closed his eyes and beat his wings as hard as he could to stop their fall. His muscles burned with effort while he suppressed the urge to roar furiously at being all but thrown out of the sky.

Their descent slowed then stopped. For a moment, he hung suspended in the air before his wings pushed them upwards.

Panting, Chace slowed his movement. He had Skylar, but she wasn't moving. With effort, he circled the spot where Gunner and Mason were waiting. Reaching the ground, he gently released Skylar and landed beside her.

Mason and Gunner raced to them. The black cat was still, and Chace nudged her, worried.

"Stop." Gunner pushed his large muzzle away and bent over to place his ear to Skylar's nose. "She's not breathing."

Chace paced. His head shot up when the scent of griffin reached him. Alert for any sign of Dillon, he was half-aware of Gunner and Mason discussing what to do with the unconscious lion.

One of the dragons landed a short distance away, followed by a few more.

Chace glanced at them, not at all convinced he had any standing among the creatures. The purple one he knew as Hala approached. She gave a small, formal bow, folding one leg beneath her.

Leery of the dragons that had no qualms about letting Freyja take Skylar, Chace hesitated, and then growled.

Griffins. He didn't know if the dragons were able to hear him. He'd never known them to exist, before meeting Skylar's father, Gavin.

Hala bowed once more. Seconds later, all of them took flight, moving like a flock towards the direction from which he smelled the griffins.

A cough came from behind him, followed by a mewling cry.

He whirled to see the lioness batting at Gunner, who was straightening a leg that was clearly broken.

"You want it fixed, keep still!" Gunner snapped in return.

Skylar responded by trying to get to her feet.

"She's a bit fucked up," Mason said, frowning. "You both are."

Chace shook his head and moved closer, nudging Skylar back to a sitting position. She growled and batted at him, too, but he pushed her onto her back with his muzzle, enjoying the tickle of her fur against his sensitive nose.

She grumbled but was still, understanding his message. She gripped his muzzle clumsily with massive paws and licked him.

He sneezed.

"That's just weird," Gunner said, watching.

Mason chuckled.

"I gotta fix that leg, Skylar."

Chace shook the paws free of his face and straightened, attention shifting to the direction where he sensed Dillon was. He moved away, determined to end this night with both their enemies neutralized.

He walked to the top of the small hill they'd taken cover behind earlier when searching for Skylar and paused, attention on the fire just beyond the caverns.

Farewell, Freyja, he said silently to the dead dragon whose body was lighting up the night.

Mason – now in his great cat form – sat on his haunches beside him. Chace glanced at him, not trusting anyone associated with Dillon and Freyja but forced to admit that the lion had thus far come in pretty handy.

Dillon was out there somewhere. Chace doubted the griffin was going to face a team of nocturnal dragons at night, if Chace didn't bring the fight to him.

Not going through another mess like The Field, he thought to himself, recalling how badly their first attempt at confronting the griffin leader had ended up. No, tonight, Dillon was going down.

Chace lifted himself into the air, following the scent of griffins. The dragons ahead of him were doing the same, and dread sank into his stomach.

The griffins emerging from the cavern outnumbered the dragons by two to one. Pausing to think, Chace altered his direction, heading towards the cavern where he sensed Dillon, instead of pursuing the other griffins. The dragons could distract the others. Once he took care of their leader, the griffins would fall in line or be slaughtered in place.

No more lassos. Now that he knew what the hibernation tools were made out of – the blood and hair of Protectors like Skylar - he made a mental note to tell Skylar they were going to use a different means of controlling those members of the shifter society that tried to rebel.

Fire exploded in the sky as the line of dragons met the griffins.

With some reluctance, Chace landed beside the hole leading into the cavern. Mason raced to meet him, and Chace tossed his head towards the dragons battling griffins. They'd need all the help they could get, and Mason was more than capable of taking out any winged creature that got too close to the ground.

The lion sprinted towards the battle while Chace dropped into the dark hole of the cavern, intent on pursuing Dillon. His wings caught him, and he lowered himself to the ground. The cavern was like an echo chamber; it was hard for him to determine the direction of the sounds he heard, but he was able to see Dillon.

The shifter was in human form, standing with a flashlight at one end of the cavern.

"Shift, dragon," Dillon ordered. "Unless you're going to snap me up right here?"

Chace growled, tempted to turn the man before him into fried chicken, the way Skylar used to accuse him of doing. If nothing else, he knew he'd win hands down no matter whether the fight was fair or not. If Dillon wanted to give his last words, Chace would humor him.

Then snap him in two.

He transformed out of his dragon form. Dillon stayed in place.

In human form, he lost the sense of how large the caverns were. Fire blazed overhead through the opening as dragons and griffins fought.

"I thought I'd offer you a deal," Dillon started.

Chace raised an eyebrow but managed to keep quiet.

"You took care of Freyja. I think that leaves room for us to negotiate."

"Go on," Chace said slowly. He folded his arms across his chest, not understanding how Dillon thought he had any kind of leverage to negotiate right now. He still tasted blood in his mouth and spit to clear it. As a dragon, he didn't mind eating raw meat. As a human, it was a little less appealing.

"Griffins and dragons can live in peace."

"Yeah, I believe that," Chace agreed. "There's one true leader of the community."

"You?" Dillon scoffed.

"Sky."

The griffin shifter rolled his eyes. "I didn't expect you to be pussy-whipped so quickly, though I guess I almost understand. She is good in the sack."

Chace's jaw clenched. He'd baited Dillon this way before and wasn't about to be drawn in.

"I know what's good for the community," he said instead. "She's good for it. She's got the right instincts, instincts creatures like you and me don't have. She's capable of compassion. And mercy."

Dillon shifted, hearing the veiled threat. "But you believe we can live in peace."

With you gone. "I do. Which is why I'll give you a choice, Dillon. Hibernation or death."

Dillon's sneer faded.

Chace waited, hoping the griffin didn't choose hibernation, not after all the damage he'd done. If the griffins had a sliver of hope that their leader could be brought back, they'd be more difficult to deal with.

"How about a challenge? You and me. To the death," Dillon suggested.

Chace assessed his body. He was exhausted from the wear and tear of his rough day, but he guessed Dillon wasn't in much better shape, after fighting his way through the dragons earlier.

"Sure," he decided. "Let's finish this."

"Sounds like a plan."

Piece of cake, Chace thought to himself and knelt, preparing to shift.

Chapter Fourteen

SKYLAR BUNNY KICKED GUNNER AWAY from her hurt leg once more, not wanting to lie still when a battle raged on. Her head pounded from oxygen depletion while her body ached. Her ribs felt bruised after Freyja's rough treatment and her broken leg was completely numb.

"Would you stop?" he growled, pushing her back. "You're not going anywhere, especially since you don't even have the energy to shift back!"

She sighed and rested her large lioness head on the ground, irritated but aware he was right. She'd tried twice to shift with no luck. Her body was just too beat up.

Dear god – please tell me I'm not stuck as a lion forever! Lying still for a moment, she stared into the direction Chace had gone, towards the flames and screeches of griffins in battle a short distance away.

It didn't take a genius to know he was going after Dillon. She wasn't able to ask about what happened to Freyja, though a peek at her Protector instincts told her the deceitful dragon was dead.

"He took out Freyja," Gunner said, as if reading her mind. "No idea what that bitch was doing. Took you almost into space before Chace threw her out of the sky."

Skylar twisted to stare at the stars overhead, unable to imagine a dragon flying in space. It made her want to laugh.

She snorted and flicked her tail. Gunner muttered and pushed the tail aside. He was handling her leg with the gentleness of a blind doctor who had no feeling in his hands.

Pain shot through her. She growled at him in warning.

"You're fine," he replied. "I have to set this. It'll hurt. I'll keep talking. Focus on my voice."

Skylar squeezed her eyes closed and braced herself for the pain.

"He killed Freyja in midair. Grabbed her by the throat."

Agony shot through her.

Skylar roared.

Gunner continued talking, unaffected. "Then he bit off her leg to get to you and saved you. Freyja fell, though I'm pretty sure she was dead before she hit the ground."

Blackness crept up on her as he continued to work with the broken leg. Skylar lay limply, close to passing out. She listened to Gunner's voice. The images in her mind created by his words were disturbing. As much as she knew Freyja was a lost cause, she didn't like the idea of any creature suffering. Even those that deserved it.

Then again, if she killed my mom ... Dillon's claims continued to replay in her mind. That her mother might've been alive less than twelve hours before ... that Skylar had almost found her or at least, was close ... that she'd ultimately failed. Her family had sacrificed itself for her. *Maybe I don't pity Freyja. I just wish I knew the truth.*

She dozed involuntarily, aware of her surroundings yet unable to wake up fully.

"Would you tell your tail to knock it off?" Gunner's annoyed voice drew her from the darkness and her thoughts.

Skylar lifted her head to see her tail smacking him repeatedly in the face. She ordered the wild appendage to stop, and it dropped, its tip still flicking. There were few things as fascinating as a tail.

The panther shifter finished a makeshift split and taped up her leg to keep it in place.

Skylar sat up, unable to quell the urge to be where the action was, to make sure Chace was alive and well. She sensed him with Dillon, and the idea the two might be fighting made her anxious to help. After all she'd been through, she wasn't about to lose her Chace, her only remaining family member.

Gunner slapped her rump and stood. "Not quite good as new. When you're ready to shift, we'll have to re-tape it."

She climbed to her feet wearily, wanting nothing better than to call the cabin and take a nap. Their night, however, was just beginning. The bandaged leg was too stiff for her to move at more than a light trot, but the pain had lessened.

Skylar walked around the rise where they'd taken refuge from the battle and took in the sight before her.

Dragon and griffins battled in the skies. The massive form of Mason was leaping and batting at any griffin that came within a few feet of him. At least one dark form of a griffin was near him, evidence of how dangerous the earthbound cat was. As she watched, at least one creature from each side fell and slammed into the ground. She flinched, her heart hurting for the creatures she was charged with protecting. They were so beautiful and lethal – yet mortal. *This* was what she was supposed to prevent.

Guilty, restless, agitated, she started forward as quickly as her leg would let her. Hearing the soft steps of a feline pursuing, she looked over her shoulder to see Gunner in his tan panther form, loping after her. He swatted at her and slowed, growling.

She understood he was doing what he thought was best, but it made her feel worse, knowing another life was in potential danger.

They trotted together towards the gaping hole in the ground that led to the caverns below.

As entrancing as the battle between creatures in the sky was, it was the one on the ground that soon drew her attention. There was no overlooking the forms of Chace and Dillon, who were each one and a half times larger than the next largest dragon or griffin shifter.

The two were in all out war, the massive creatures bounding

effortlessly between the earth and sky. They maneuvered around the battling griffins and dragons as if the others were standing still, landed lightly atop hills only to bounce into the sky again, soar towards the stars then plummet to the earth and land lightly.

Their acrobatics were more incredible than anything she'd seen, and she couldn't help thinking that she had a lot to learn about being a shifter.

Both beasts were bleeding, though it didn't seem to slow them. Dillon appeared to be trying to wear the bigger dragon pursuing him down with the sky sprints and gravity defying maneuvers.

Chace not only kept up with apparent ease, but he also managed to slash Dillon more often than the griffin was able to wound him.

Skylar winced as Chace's talons shredded one of Dillon's wings. As much as the griffin deserved all the pain in the world, she just couldn't bring herself to feel triumph seeing him being beaten to death slowly. She had no doubt Chace would win. The dragon shifter had been reborn, and the intensity and viciousness of his strikes showed her what his intention was this night.

No longer able to take refuge in the sky, Dillon turned on Chace, his dangerous tail poised to strike.

I hate that thing, she thought, recalling how much damage the whip-like tail was capable of inflicting. Skylar trotted towards them, Gunner beside her. The ground trembled as Dillon flung Chace to the ground. The dragon hopped to his feet and shredded Dillon's other wing, eliciting a scream of pain and fury from the griffin.

Skylar hurried as fast as she could go, hobbling towards the battling beasts. She wanted to be there if Chace needed her, even if she doubted she had the motor skills needed yet to do much more than become a speed bump for the enraged griffin.

Testing her magic, she was able to feel the different signatures of shifters but not yet pull one to her. Her short down time with Gunner had renewed some of her strength, but she guessed it'd take a good night of sleep and a full-blown buffet for her to have the energy to shift.

The closer she got, the slower she went. Every time one of the great beasts threw the other down, the earth shook. Skylar eyed the opening to the caverns, not about to get close enough to fall in with the ground moving beneath her.

Dillon and Chace toppled to the ground, grappling in a confusing jumble of wings, legs and tails. Roars and squawks filled the air, along with the occasional grunt and crunch of rocks and boulders that exploded beneath their combined weight. Sand was kicked up into the air, and Skylar sneezed as a cloud of dust settled over her.

She stopped, watching, unable to tell what was going on as the two rolled and wrestled. Fire blew by Dillon's head and was followed by a bellow of pain from Chace, as if Dillon had bitten him.

They stopped moving, limbs and wings and heads all locked in place in a silent battle of brute strength, like two wrestlers at a draw. Only Dillon's tail was flying, trying to grab Chace's legs or wind around his neck.

Skylar eyed it, the sudden urge to snatch the flailing, dangerous tail enhanced by a feline's predatory instinct. She approached more cautiously, taking in the two. Both were straining, the scent of charred fur, blood and sweat in the air. Her nose wrinkled at the power of the smells, and she crept closer silently. Chace was on top of the griffin, but his head and neck were trapped beneath it, creating an awkward position for both of them.

Dillon's leg lashed out reflexively as he lost his grip on Chace's neck. It smacked into Skylar and sent her tumbling back.

She landed on the side with her hurt leg and growled in pain. The splint had snapped, leaving tape clinging to her limb. Standing with effort, she tossed dirt from her small mane then moved forward again.

The two hadn't changed position. Dillon regained his grip, while Chace's muscles bulged as he strained to break away. Dillon's tail was prodding different spots, trying to find a way between their bodies to grab Chace.

Skylar moved as closed as she dared, watching the tail carefully.

When certain she could predict where it'd go next, she crouched.

One. Two. Three. She leapt at it, landing on top of the two beasts. Skylar batted the tail then bit down on it hard.

Dillon shrieked and released Chace.

The two creatures rolled a part, and Skylar toppled off them, landing too close to Dillon for comfort. She got to her feet and found herself facing the angry, injured griffin. Before she was able to react, he smashed a leg into her, sending her sprawling once more.

A feline roar drew Dillon's attention, and Gunner launched at the griffin. He sank claws into Dillon's flank and tore open gaping wounds. Dillon rounded on the panther and knocked him down with one blow, preparing to snap Gunner's head off.

Skylar started forward, only for someone to plant a massive paw on her tail. Spinning, she saw Chace directly behind her. He released her and nudged her out of the way gently with a bloodied muzzle.

Understanding his nonverbal command, she stepped aside to give him room to attack Dillon.

With speed that astounded her, the massive teal dragon closed the distance between him and the griffin in a blur. She heard his talons shred through Dillon a split second before the sound of his fangs sinking into the griffin's neck.

A sickening crack filled the air, and Skylar flinched.

Dillon went limp.

Chace shook him viciously by the neck to make certain he was dead then flung him aside.

Gunner was bloodied and dusty but on his feet, panting.

Skylar stared at Dillon's still body. Dared she believe those responsible for destroying her family and life were now dead?

Chace's growl rumbled deep in his throat. He was breathing hard, and blood glistened on his scales in the starlight.

Skylar limped to him, unable to identify what emotions were going through her. Gratitude, hope.

Regret. So many had died, and the divide within the shifter community was deep enough that she wasn't sure how they were going to repair the trust between shifters like the griffins and Mason and those they'd captured and placed into hibernation.

Not to mention that the only two people who knew the truth about what happened to her mother were now dead.

Not sure I could've trusted their versions of events anyway. Why was it so hard to have that one question answered? She'd decided to accept the loss of a past she wasn't able to change – with the exception of her mother.

She rubbed up against one of Chace's legs. His muzzle lowered, and he nudged her again then nipped at one of her ears. He was tired, the strain clear in the tremble of his limbs.

Skylar sat beside him, gazing up at him.

The battle between the griffins and dragons still raged. Yet another issue she wasn't certain how to fix.

Chace's attention went overhead. He spread his wings and lowered his body then leapt into the air, hanging above them. With not even an ounce of gentleness, he stretched his legs to Dillon's broken body and gripped it with his talons. He hauled them both towards the heavens.

Skylar watched in fatigued curiosity. He appeared to be headed directly into the fray, clutching Dillon close to his body.

Gunner joined her. He, too, was limping and smelled of fresh blood.

Chace pushed into the middle of the battle. Skylar cried out in objection and warning, expecting the griffins to attack the man who killed their leader. As if to goad them on, Chace roared loudly enough for his cry to echo in the caverns below.

To her surprise, the battle stopped the moment the flying beasts noticed Chace. He wove deliberately among them, ensuring everyone saw Dillon's limp carcass.

Mason trotted up to her and Gunner, showing no signs of being hurt. He paced in front of them, eyes on the skies.

Skylar waited with baited breath to see what happened next.

The griffins backed off. Regrouping a short distance away, they began descending from the skies, circling then landing in a herd near the opening of the caverns.

The dragons drifted off as well, back towards the hill where Gunner had treated her. Rather than landing, they remained in the sky, circling.

Chace dropped Dillon's body into the gaping caverns then followed the other dragons. He circled downward rapidly, settling on the ground behind the hill, beyond her sight.

Skylar, Gunner and Mason hurried back towards them. She lagged behind, unable to keep up with her hurt leg. Her muscles were burning from exhaustion, her body shaking. She wanted nothing more than to crawl into bed and sleep for a year.

Hurting, Skylar slowed to a walk and reached the group last, just as the three men were pulling on their clothing. Agitated she couldn't shift, she began to wonder once more if she was doomed to remain a feline forever.

The scent of pizza drifted towards her, and she twisted to see the cabin. It had appeared silently a few feet away. Her gaze lingered on the open door, and she almost groaned at the thought of eating half a dozen pizzas then sinking into the cloud-like bed. She'd never been so thrilled by food or a nap before.

"Sky, can you shift?" Chace asked, approaching her.

She gave a mournful yowl in response and sat.

He smiled tightly, the strain of the evening showing on his features. Her withers reached his mid-chest and she lifted her head to rest it on his shoulder.

Chace chuckled warmly and hugged her to him, ruffling her thick fur. She breathed in his honey-bonfire scent. It was mixed with blood, dust and sweat and reassured her he truly was alive.

They both were. They'd managed to defeat Freyja and Dillon and survive.

"I've got to go deal with the griffins. I'm pretty sure they'll fall into line, now that Dillon is gone," Chace said into her soft fur. "I want to get this process started. When you're ... rested, we can both confront them about how things will be from now on."

Unable to speak, she opened her mouth in a loud growl.

"There's a surprise for you in the cabin," he added.

She wanted to demand to know what took him so long to show up today and why he'd run off with Freyja.

Not that it mattered, since the white dragon was dead. But she couldn't shake her irritation at feeling abandoned for a few hours.

"We'll talk later," he assured her, amused. "Then we can figure out how to clean up this mess." He moved away, determination on his features.

Skylar watched him trot away, envying his energy. She was completely sapped, her body yearning for rest.

The breeze brought the scent of pizza to her once more.

"Let me get your leg fixed again," Gunner said, starting towards her.

She snapped at him, her patience gone. Not about to let him corner her so he could torture her again, she limped quickly towards the cabin, her refuge. Head low, she climbed the first two steps before she noticed someone standing in the doorway.

Skylar froze, staring at the odd woman before her. Small, bald, slender to the point of emaciated …

Completely off her radar. If her Protector senses had anything to say about it, they'd tell her there was no one in front of her at all. Skylar sniffed at the stranger. She smelled like …

Apple pie.

There's no way … She ascended the steps so she could see the woman's face in the full light of the cabin.

"Are you Skylar?" A familiar, soft voice, one she hadn't heard in years, riveted her attention.

Skylar studied the woman before her, barely recognizing her. She was far too skinny, her exposed skin scarred and her head completely shaved.

The smell, the voice …

It can't be anyone else.

Suddenly, Chace's abrupt disappearance made sense. She'd thought him on his own agenda, maybe trying to deal with Freyja. Instead, he'd been off rescuing her mother.

"Yeah, that's Sky," Gunner said from behind her. "She's stuck. You are?"

"Ginger. Her mother." Ginger eyed Skylar with a maternally critical gaze. "You're a mess, Sky."

Was she dead? Because that was the only way it seemed possible for Ginger to be standing before her. Skylar moved forward.

"Gentle, Sky," Gunner reminded her.

"You're a big girl, aren't you?" Ginger asked, eyes glimmering with amusement and tears.

Sky stood before her, her head at the same level as her mother's. Not trusting her feline motor skills to handle the fragile woman, Skylar rubbed her cheek against Ginger's.

Her mother laughed and dug her hands into the thick fur around her neck, hugging her hard.

"I missed you, my Sky," she whispered, her warm tears reaching Skylar's skin through the fur. "I'm so glad you found your dragon."

Skylar's heart broke at the note of profound sorrow in Ginger's voice. She knew her mother was thinking of Gavin and wondered what would've happened, if both parents had been able to live.

Every muscle in her body wanted to leap for joy, but she feared frightening or hurting her mother by trying to maneuver her lioness body in for a feline hug.

Instead, Skylar stood, trembling as her mother hugged her large head and ran her fingers through her fur.

Chace found my mother. She couldn't believe it. Even smelling her mother's familiar apple pie scent and hearing her beautiful voice, Skylar almost swore this was a dream. An incredible one she didn't want to end.

She cuddled up to her mother as much as possible, wanting to hug her so badly, it hurt. Cursing her shifter blood, Skylar did her best to show her mother how happy she was, without knocking them both over. Inside, she was weeping, what few memories she could recall of her mother running through her mind in a loop.

All in a period of twenty-four hours, she and Chace had found one another again, defeated the enemies of the shifters and found her missing mother.

It was the best day of her life.

Chapter Fifteen

JUST AS THE SUNRISE CRACKED the horizon, Chace returned from the meeting with the griffins, somewhat satisfied with the results. They'd been silent when he explained the new rules and what would happen if they ever rebelled again.

Probably not an approach Skylar would appreciate. He'd immediately thrown the possibility of hibernation out the window, threatening to kill anyone who thought to follow Dillon's footsteps.

The dragons hadn't bothered to shift, when meant he'd have to track them all down one by one with Skylar to discuss the future of the shifters. They had stopped circling the area not long before his return, retreating to sleep the day away.

So much to do. He let himself feel the exhaustion of the past few days. With it, he also experienced a sense of deep pride at all they'd been through and all they'd done. He had been a selfish man his entire life, until Skylar tracked him down. Now, he understood what it was to think outside of his world. He didn't have the same tact for compassion she did, but he had figured out the greater purpose of his life: to protect and lead the shifter community, beside the beautiful other half of his heart.

The cool chill before dawn made him shiver as he walked around the hill behind which his cabin stood. A bonfire was burning a few meters away, with Gunner and a few others seated around it. Chace went to them, wanting to give Skylar and her mother time to catch up before he started to figure out what to do with a mother-in-law.

"Tea?" Gunner offered, holding out a cup.

Chace shook his head in response. His gaze drifted to the cabin, and he snorted. Four of the feline shifters in their cat forms, including Mason, were curled up on the porch, sleeping. The cabin had put out a space heater for them.

"Damn cabin," he mumbled with some affection. "Still throwing all my clothes on the floor but puts out a heater for the strays."

Gunner smiled.

Chace sank down into a sit close to his best friend, soon mesmerized by the warmth and dance of the bonfire.

"How you holding up?" Gunner asked.

"Great. Don't need any of your evil doctor magic."

Gunner laughed. "It's about surviving. You don't have to like the experience to get through it."

"Yeah," Chace agreed with a sigh. "Feels like there's so much to do."

"The danger is over, though. The rest will heal with time."

"No offense, but you are the worst doctor ever."

Gunner winked.

Chace wasn't certain what that meant, unless his friend was indirectly admitting to being a dick on purpose, another man out to teach him a lesson.

"Thank you," he said. "For climbing mountains with me, nursing me back to health, and putting up with me for a few hundred years."

"I always knew the potential was there. You just had to grow up a little. Besides, you always made me laugh," Gunner added. "But you're welcome, Chace. You're a better friend than you know."

Hardly. Chace said nothing, content to relax beside the fire with his longtime friend.

"Hey."

His heart skipped a beat, and his gaze flew up at Skylar's voice.

For a moment, he wasn't able to respond. She absolutely glowed with happiness, her eyes bright and her face flushed. She'd never been so beautiful. Skylar wore his sweats and a jacket, her mussed hair down around her shoulders and her feet in flip-flops.

"Hey," he managed at last. He patted the spot beside him.

She sat, her peachy, clean scent stirring his blood. "So ... you ran away and found my mom."

Chace laughed at her cool tone.

She looked at him, the excitement in her face. Unable to help himself, he cupped her cheeks in his hands and kissed her lightly.

"Glad to see you're not a cat anymore," he teased.

"Omigod. It took hours for me to be able to shift back," she said with a sigh. A troubled look crossed her features. "Mom told me what they did to her."

"No one will hurt either of you again, Sky," he said softly. "I swear it."

"I know." She met his gaze, jumbled emotions crossing her features. She gripped one of his arms and leaned into him. "I told her we'd protect her, along with the rest of the shifters."

He planted a warm kiss on her forehead.

"We've got a long path ahead of us, don't we? Fixing the mess Freyja and Dillon made." She considered.

"We can do it."

"Yeah, we can." A smile replaced her concern. "My god, Chace. I didn't think you could be any more incredible, and then you go and rescue my mom. It just makes me want to ... ugh!" She shoved him onto his back, landing on top of him. Skylar began fluttering hot little kisses across his face and neck.

Chace laughed at the tickling sensation and wrapped his arms around her, rolling her onto her back. He settled on top of her, between her thighs, his arousal growing hard.

"I love you," she whispered, tears sliding down her cheeks. "Thank you, Chace."

He gave her a long, lingering kiss, one that reignited the tired fire in his blood.

"Uh, guys." Gunner cleared his throat. "Take it somewhere else."

Chace broke off the kiss, his blood burning with need. "Show me," he whispered for her ears only.

Skylar's face broke into a smile.

He rolled off her and pulled her to her feet.

She snatched his hand and ran, tugging him with her. Laughing the entire time, Skylar tugged him far enough away that no one could hear their lovemaking then spun, wrapping her arms around his neck and launching herself onto his hips.

She rained kisses all over his face, her thighs gripping him tightly.

He knelt and gently laid her on her back, claiming her mouth hungrily. Chace pulled off her shirt and pants roughly then his own, desperate to feel her skin against his once more and to experience every inch of her body. When he settled between her legs, they both groaned.

"I never thought we'd be here like this," she said, taking his face in her hands.

"About to get sand shoved into every crevice of our bodies?" he teased.

"Totally worth it!" She giggled. "I mean *here*. Starting our lives together. Taking care of the shifters. Being a family."

Family. A word he'd never really understood until her. Chace smiled, loving her enthusiasm and happiness.

"I owe you so much," she said, her voice catching. "My mother …" She stopped, tears streaming down her face.

"You owe me nothing, Sky," he murmured. "You showed me what it is to love and be loved. I can't ever repay you for those lessons. After we spend some time together, we'll all three of us go out on that pizza date I owe you. Okay?"

She nodded, unable to talk. His desire was spinning out of control quickly.

"I need you. I want you. I love you so much, Sky," he whispered into her hair, his urgency rising. "Sky, I need to be inside you."

"Show me," she managed in a barely audible voice.

"I will. Every day of our lives."

She sighed.

He plunged into her hot, slick depths, and she gasped, arching beneath him.

This is where I belong. She is my home. Chace squeezed his eyes closed and buried his face in the nape of her neck. She was right. Today was the beginning of their forever, and god help him, he was completely lost to his other half, the one woman who made his life worth living.

My heart, my soul, my Sky.

Heart of Fire

ABOUT THE AUTHOR

Lizzy Ford is the author of over twenty books written for young adult and adult paranormal romance readers, to include the internationally bestselling "Rhyn Trilogy," "Witchling Series" and the "War of Gods" series. Considered a freak of nature by her peers for the ability to write and release a commercial quality novel in under a month, Lizzy has focused on keeping her readers happy by producing brilliant, gritty romances that remind people why true love is a trial worth enduring.

Lizzy's books can be found on every major ereader library, to include: Amazon, Barnes and Noble, iBooks, Kobo, Sony and Smashwords. She lives in southern Arizona with her husband, three dogs and a cat.

Connect with Lizzy:

WEBSITE:
www.GuerrillaWordfare.com

FACEBOOK:
www.Facebook.com/LizzyFordBooks

or find her on TWITTER!
@LizzyFord2010

Made in the USA
Charleston, SC
07 May 2014